I DO

Tales of Relationships

by

B R Johnson

I DO

Tales of Relationships

Copyright © by B R Johnson 2015

Having lived in south GA all my life, I have taken the liberty of inventing landmarks, restaurants, and other places which were not present in these parts during the time these stories take place.

Table Contents

For the boys in my life,
Bill, Dave, Wayne, and Ben,
the four of whom guaranteed
my life was never boring.

INTRODUCTION

First let me say this collection contains some stories about spousal and/or child abuse. Many people find it difficult to read about the subject. I said this up front because I don't want this to come as a shock to those folks when reading my work for the first time. I can also say that my novel, when it comes out in a few months, does not.

This collection of short stories started many years ago while I attended college the first time. I continued to play around with them for years while I worked, attended college on the 'finish by forty plan,' continued to obtain a Master's Degree and get remarried. Only one of the stories in this book ever saw the light of day. The short story entitled, The Beginning, won a pen award contest in a professional newsletter many, many years ago and is being reproduced here after being revised.

Work, a new marriage, a new son . . . . Most of you will be able to identify with real life getting in way of things you have planned for your life.

After my retirement, some years ago, I decided to write a novel. Having no idea how long, how many words, a novel should contain, I over-wrote by at least a couple of hundred thousand words. I still had more than enough for two novels. I realized, after joining an on-line critique group, I needed to cut it by more than half. I also needed some folks who knew what they were doing to assist me. I needed to develop a thick-skin, put my writing out there for others who knew a lot more about writing than I did to read and critique, and help me along the way.

The on-line critique group, Critique Circle, taught me I had some good things to say, but needed to get better at putting them on paper. I took some licks from them, but knew I needed even more help, so I joined a local writers' group.

This local writers' group flayed me, but convinced me to keep trying. I can't thank them enough for their encouragement. I'm even more thankful I joined the on-line group first. I got my hurt feelings out of the way in the privacy of my own home and I was ready to listen to the constructive criticism of the local group. Some of these stories were critiqued by both groups, some by only one, some by neither.

Welcome to each of you reading this collection; I thank you.

These stories are not at all like the novels I'm writing. Please leave your comments on Amazon or on my author's page there, or B R Johnson's author page on Facebook.

LAST TIMES

"When was the last time you had a chocolate milkshake?" Andrew asked.

"Hell, I don't know," Paul answered. "Since they told me I had diabetes, they ain't let me have nothing that tasted good."

"When was the last time you slept with a woman?"

"Well, hell, I slept with my wife a lot of years, but I don't 'member the last time I had sex if that's what you're asking," Paul replied.

"Yeah, that's what I thought," Andrew said, disgusted. "Me, neither. I was just setting out here by myself and you come out here and set down. Thinking about the last times I done a lot of things. Thought I'd ask you 'bout last times. You don't remember any better than me, do you?"

"Well, hell, Andrew, the thing about last times is by the time you realize it was the last time, it's been so damn long, you done plum forgot when, and can't even remember it was the last time. Sometimes, things're worth remembering, like the last time you had sex, you might remember who, but you might not remember when. Now, the last time for a chocolate milkshake, well that ain't even worth remembering, not like sex anyway."

They sat on the porch of the Heritage House Nursing Home watching traffic and talking a little. It might not be the best nursing home in town, they didn't know, but at least they had interesting traffic. Ambulances coming and going from the hospital, and fire trucks sometimes. College students walking back and forth, and in good weather they complained about the way the college girls dressed.

The ugly nurse came to get the men from the porch; they knew it was the ugly nurse because the pretty one had on blue scrubs today. The ugly one wore pink. They didn't even bother looking up beyond the color.

"Come on, Mr. Andrew," the ugly one said. "Let's go in. Time for your supper. Tonight you get to sit with the pretty ladies." She turned his wheelchair and bumped him over the threshold and into the hallway, scurrying to the dining room. Paul followed on his walker.

Andrew smiled when he got to the table; the ugly one had indeed put him at the table with the pretty ladies. They spread the men out among the tables since there were fewer of them than women, and the women complained if the men congregated separately. This was the table with the ladies who bothered to put on bras, a little lipstick, and smiles when they got to have a man at their table.

"Good evening, Andrew," they all twittered. "How are you this evening?"

"Fine as frog's hair, ladies," he responded with a

smile, tipping a non-existent hat. "What's for dinner this evening?"

"I think it's meatloaf again," Gladys said, "but it's not so bad, I've had worse in my time."

"I don't know," Beatrice complained. "Pretty awful, if you ask me. I always made mine with brown gravy. This stuff's made with ketchup."

"The potatoes are usually good. I think they use real potatoes," Gladys said "And the green beans are always good."

"The green beans're always overcooked," Myrtle complained. "They should still have some snap. These are always mushy."

"That's how we cooked them in the south," Gladys said. "Where did you say you grew up, Andrew?"

"Right here in south Georgia," Andrew answered, looking at Gladys with renewed interest. She was the only one of the ladies not complaining about everything on the table. Nice to hear some pleasantries.

After supper, Andrew wheeled his chair beside Gladys in the television room. He tentatively put his hand on her arm. "Would you like to sit on the porch with me a while?"

She looked at him in mild surprise. "I think I'd like that, Andrew." She stood and pushed his wheelchair to the porch.

They sat, talking a little, about their childhoods, their deceased spouses, their children, some also deceased. Neither had visitors very often. They grew up only a few miles apart, but those days a few miles was now like hundreds or thousands. They discussed how their children scattered as soon as they were grown.

Paul came out to join them for a while, but didn't stay long when he saw they were engrossed in each other's conversation and didn't want to talk to him.

"When was the last time you went to the beach, or heard the ocean?" Andrew asked.

"You know, Andrew. It's been a couple of years, at least, since they took us on a trip down to Panama City. Would be nice to go again, don't you think?"

"I think it was about four or five years ago," he answered, shaking his head. "I'd like to watch the waves again. I used to like the beach."

When the blue-scrubbed nurse came to remind them it was time for the outside doors to be closed, they went inside. Each went to their own rooms to prepare for bed.

Things settled down for the evening and most of the residents were in bed, and there came a quiet knock on her door. Gladys knew without asking who it was and got up to open it for him. Andrew wheeled himself in and closed the door behind him.

"When was the last time you slept with a man's

arms around you?" he asked.

"A very long time. But you know, even an old woman is still a woman."

He stood and took the few wobbling steps to her bed. Maybe this wouldn't yet be the last time.

THE HAIRCUT

"You know, that boy of yourn would be perfect, if only he'd get a haircut," her oldest aunt, Roxie said.

"Yes ma'am, I know, aunt Roxie," Lulu said with a sigh. "He's 'bout as close as he's ever gonna get, I 'spect."

Lulu went about wiping down the long kitchen table, getting ready to lay out the Sunday dinner for everyone.
Davis came through the back door with serving dishes stored on an enclosed back porch. He grinned at his mother, shaking his head, put several dishes on the counter beside the sink, and began setting the table.

"In my day, we didn't have no trouble gettin' a youngun to do what they was told," Aunt Viney said. "Why my Henry just took the strop, and they wasn't no arguin' with 'em."

Lulu patted Davis on the back and handed him a fistful of forks for the table. They glanced at each other without speaking. She began gathering food from the stove, and after placing forks, he came to help.

All six old aunts got into the discussion while Lulu and Davis continued setting food on the table, made glasses of iced tea, and dragged in extra chairs.

"Davis, go tell the younguns to come fix their

plates. Let's get them out of the way before we sit down to eat," Lulu said. "Ask Uncle Clyde to come in and say grace."

"Yes, ma'am."

"Bless this food, Lord," Uncle Clyde intoned, as Lulu put herself close to the smallest children. "Bless the ladies who prepared it for us. Bless this food for the nourishment of our bodies and our bodies for our service to our Lord. Bless our service men wherever they may be, Lord. Keep them save. . . ." His voice went on for at least five minutes.

Lulu put her hands on the small children several times to keep them quiet, thankful when Uncle Clyde finally said, "Amen."

Mothers began filling plates for their children from the dishes lined on the counter. Teenagers pushed their way to the front of the line. Their mothers smoothly steered them back. The oldest aunts and uncles saw no need to move or get out of way of the mothers, children, or teenagers, obliged to fill plates around them.

Lulu walked around the table, filling glasses, waiting on aunts, uncles and her mother. "Can I get you some more tea, Uncle Clyde?"

"Just a little."

"I'd like some more of those peas, Lulu," Aunt Maud called, from the other end of the table.

"Yes, ma'am."

"Did you make another pan of cornbread, Lulu?"

"Yes, I did. Should be coming out of the oven any minute now."

"I'll check on it, Mama," Davis said, opening the oven, pulling out a cast iron skillet. "Biscuits are ready, too." He made quick work of slicing cornbread, putting the plate on the table, dumping biscuits into a basket already there.

"Thank you, son."

Alone after everyone left the big kitchen, Davis asked, "Mama, why do you do this to yourself every month?"

"Because family is important. If I don't, nobody will."

"But you work yourself to death for days and I don't see anybody appreciates it."

"They really do. Old people just don't show it."

"Okay, I'll take your word. You cook for days and they bring one dish, or nothing. Somehow it doesn't seem fair to me."

"It's okay, if I get tired, I'll quit. You're just tired of them fussing about your hair," she teased him.

"If I didn't get tired of your fussing, their fussing

once a month won't touch me," he joked back at her.

His hair allowed to dry naturally, hung down his back in ringlets. But he hated the curls, so he used a brush vigorously with a blow dryer in a vain attempt to straighten it.

His mother had argued and threatened to cut it in his sleep when he first refused to cut it. No amount of persuasion or old fashioned argument would change his mind.

All her arguments dispelled as he got a job in spite of the long hair. He had more

girlfriends than she liked, and he didn't get arrested for being on the streets.

He never rebelled against her tirades, going about being the same polite and respectful boy he had always been, growing into a man. All her friends spoke highly of him, but ended any statement about him with a disclaimer: but he would be perfect if only he would cut his hair.

Always the first, usually the only, grandchild to visit his grandmother after his grandfather died in his sleep. He often used his only day off each week to help her clean her yards just as his grandfather had. It distressed her to see them with small limbs from the pecan, oak and pine trees, and the grass overgrown.

Davis, not a brilliant student, persevered through high school while working a full time job. He didn't ask for money for school or the clunker he drove.

When it quit running, as it often did, he rode an old bicycle until he saved enough money for repairs.

Months turned into years, (slowly for him, quickly for her) his mother still took every opportunity to rant or get in little comments. Lulu refused to see the good qualities, she did not see beyond the wild bushy mop flying about his head. He got into a habit of pulling it back in a ponytail low on his neck when around his mother. When she fussed or commented, he did not respond. Three years after the saga began, he still didn't get a haircut except for an occasional trim of split ends.

Lulu heard on the radio of some boys who got arrested for having drugs on campus of his high school. Over the months, she heard of teenagers killed joyriding in a stolen car. She heard of boys whose parents went to Texas to pick them up after they stole, and wrecked, a vehicle from one of the fathers. She heard of boys arrested for being drunk on the main streets of their little town. But her son continued to be the same polite and respectful boy he had always been growing into a man.

When her oldest living uncle died, all the great nephews asked to be pallbearers. None of the boys had ever done this before. None refused, but all were apprehensive. Davis pulled his hair back into his now-familiar ponytail and led the other boys through the proceedings as though he had always been the leader.

Uncle Manfred's wife, Aunt Annabelle, was a very out-spoken lady. The family sat around the house after the funeral; no one wanted to be first to leave. Old people wandered the rooms, wanting to leave, wanting a nap, their usual custom, but more, wanting to escape thoughts of their own mortality.

Davis went about making plates of desserts for the old people, glasses of iced tea. He reminded the other young people to get up and give their chairs to the old people, took babies to bedrooms and laid them down for naps, sang to them until they slept. He found places for the older relatives who needed naps, covered their feet, if they needed. He cautioned children playing outside to go to the other side of the house to play. He told the teenagers sneaking a cigarette out by the shed they could be seen from the kitchen window.

Aunt Annabelle spotted the ponytail tucked out of the way down the collar of Davis' shirt. She began the familiar tirade about young people of the day, with long hair, dope heads and wild and crazy. No children of her generation dared wear their hair that long and if they dared, well, their parents put an end to it.

Lulu listened to the tirade and thought about his actions the past several hours. She began to get angry. She had raised this boy to be polite and respectful. Now criticized without regard for the kind of man he was. As usual, Davis said nothing beyond asking if he could get a cold drink for anyone. His mother walked to him, put her arm around his waist, gave a small hug, and turned.

"Aunt Annabelle, I think it's time we all started

12

seeing my Davis for the man he is, not just for his hair. Other than me, has anyone else here offered to give you his chair, or find you a place to take a nap? Davis is the only one here with any manners, or didn't any of you notice? No other young folks here offered to fix a plate, make a drink, wash a dish, or help in any way. Not even your own grandchildren."

"It's okay, Mama," Davis said. He hugged her, patted her back, and went about making a glass of iced tea with extra sugar for Aunt Annabelle.

THE BEGINNING

He raised his hand to slap the child again, and the sound of screams pierced his ears like knives. He looked at the marks on her face, and fell to the floor with an anguished cry.

"Oh, God, what have I done?"

His wife grabbed their child, wrapping her arms around the tiny girl. "Get out!" She shrieked. "Damn it, Aaron, get out." The fear and hatred on their faces tore at his heart, and he knew he had to do something.

From his position on the floor, his arms reached out to them, but Nicole pulled the girl away. Rosie still cried as her mother held her, and he stared in horror at the damage done to them.

When laid off from his job three months before, he had been sure it would only be a short time until he was working again. But things were tough all over, and everywhere he went, he got the same answer. Sorry, no jobs available now, come back later. Some didn't even bother with that offer.

His unemployment compensation payments barely covered the rent and utilities, other bills unpaid. First, the gas, but it was spring and they didn't need heat. Cable television, and the telephone. No more Friday night trips to Pizza Hut, no Sunday afternoon movies, even at the cheap theater.

Nicole's mother never tired of reminding her she tried to stop her from marrying this high school dropout. She never mentioned Nicole also dropped out.

So much in love, they couldn't wait for maturity to prove their love. She became pregnant half way through their junior year in high school. They both quit school to get married.

He worked full time at Mack's Service Station. Only minimum wage, but they were in love and the tiny apartment, the furniture from the Salvation Army Thrift Store, and Goodwill, didn't matter. Both worked to make the dingy apartment a home.

It took two years to pay off the medical bills from the birth of their daughter, but their love and Rosie made a good life. Never any extra money. She tried to work, but the high cost of child care and the part time jobs she could find made it impossible. The old car sometimes wouldn't run. They agreed Nicole would stay home, maybe keep someone else's child to help pay bills.

Now, at the end of his rope. Frustration of getting past due bills they couldn't pay hit him

hard when she told him she applied for food stamps. She dropped the bombshell.

"I'm pregnant," she whispered.

Without a thought, his hand flew out slapped her. Never before, would have sworn he never would.

But he did and it relieved the frustration - it felt good. He slapped her again.

She screamed and cried for him to stop as their tiny Rosie ran into the room screaming, grabbing his leg.

He instinctively pushed the child away and as he did, she cried, "You leave my mama alone."

His own pent-up fears and emotions boiled in him, and he hit her twice before the sound of her piercing screams brought him to his senses.

Aaron watched Nicole hold their beloved Rosie, the hurt and fear in their eyes as they looked at him.

The pain in his heart more than he could bear, he pushed himself up, turned, and ran from the small apartment.

THE HOUSE

The whimpering child woke her. She held him to her bosom and hummed the same wordless tune used to calm him every day, while she lay gathering her thoughts. Rocking gently, back and forth, back and forth, always calmed him. The child settled, as he usually did, and they drifted back into a restless sleep.

The woman awoke again when the only rooster left in the woods nearby began to crow. Trying to ease away from the child and rise, he missed the warmth of her body and stirred. She reached out, rubbed his back, and he quieted. She sat by the window and watched the sky brighten. Within a few minutes the child awoke and whimpered until he saw her. She smiled to reassure him but felt no assurance herself.

"I'm hungry," he whined, as he climbed into her lap.

"Come," she said quietly, and led him to the table in the corner which held a pitcher and wash bowl, poured a little water into the bowl, and washed sleep from their eyes. There was little to eat, but maybe there would be enough for the boy.

On the table in the kitchen, as usual, a plate with a sandwich, wrapped in waxed paper, made with soft white bread. Milk set in a small container, enough for the boy. Soon the people would come and once again they would run to hide. Done with his meager breakfast, they went out the back door into the area which used to thrive as a small kitchen garden.

As she sat on a wide covered bench in the gazebo, the boy ran and chased at shadows in the small enclosed area. Another hot day and she dreaded keeping the boy quiet in the stifling small attic room. Running and playing with small sticks, he kept coming to put his head in her lap then ran to play again. He played loudly by himself, probably, she thought, because he had to be so quiet during the day.

As every day, while she sat and watched the boy play, she thought about events which brought them to this life. The soldiers, a long time gone, how long she couldn't remember, destroyed everything except this house.

At some time, the house being repaired, workmen had been all around for a long time. That time had been much more difficult than now. Those men came into the small attic room, and everywhere else in the house. The house was wonderful when finished. The house looked as it did when she came as a young bride.

Columns on the front porch restored and no longer showed signs of the marks left by the games of the many children who used to play. Gone were the scuff marks left by soldier's boots and men of the family as they leaned back in huge rocking chairs and propped their feet. A fresh coat of whitewash covered the exterior of the huge house.

The most wonderous furniture placed where it belonged. Restored to its original beauty, it wore almost the same brocades as before the war.

War, she thought, what horrible destruction, and now our lives are gone. My husband, all his brothers, my precious mama, all my family. The only ones left are the boy and me. Why, she could but wonder. Why us, not important, only small players in the times, and not players in the war at all.

Soldiers had been the most frightening aspect of war, of course. All that her husband's family worked so many years for destroyed. The war took the men away; women left to carry on without their help, with no experience in running the plantation. Her husband and his father always said she, her mother-in-law, and his sisters need not worry their pretty little heads about men's work. They tried anyway, for ever so long to keep the place working.

Sounds of an automobile coming up the long driveway told her she delayed too long. She called quietly and rushed him as they ran toward the house. Their staircase door closing at their back as the door to the kitchen opened from the outside.

"This door is unlocked again," she heard as they rushed up the stairs. She heard the woman in the kitchen telling the men in uniform to look around for missing things or damage.

The boy knew the routine well, and he sped up the stairs all the way to the attic. The woman closed the door much more forcefully than she should, and leaned on it to catch her breath.

In a while, the men made a search, but they never came all the way up to the attic. She went about their daily routine of wiping the dirt from the boy and got out the books and games they would use during the day. As they settled into their routine, the boy restless, his mind would not concentrate on books, and his restlessness continued as she tried to interest him in a game.

When it came time for his daily nap, he lay down and wiggled more than his usual custom. She rubbed his back, which usually calmed him, and sang softly. She drifted off to sleep, and he squirmed away.

Before she could stop him, he scampered out the door. She jumped up, but slowed by sleepiness, she was not fast enough to catch him. He headed down the front stairs as she ran after him.

She reached him and saw the men in uniform. She grabbed the boy and held him close.
Men, coming closer!

She spotted two elderly ladies and went to them pleading. "Don't let them get the boy," she begged. Did they not hear her? They looked around as though distressed. She went to them crying, begging again for their help.

The women backed away from her and turned to another group of people she had not seen until now.

The men in uniform were closer still!

The group of people acted as though they did not hear, but felt deep distress and several began to back away and cry. Her fear and despair evident in their actions. She begged for help, and as her pleas became more urgent, many people in the group began to cry, feeling her helplessness and despair.

People backed away from the elderly ladies as though their own pain came from them. Ladies, now hysterical with grief and pain, cried and pleaded for someone to get them out of the house. She still tried to get the boy away from the men in uniform and in her panic, she ran into the midst of people.

Many of them, overcome with grief, sobbed. Men, unable to understand their feelings, pulled handkerchiefs from their pockets, and began to shed tears.

She still held the boy and begged for help against the men in uniform. Seeing the grief and sorrow in the crowd, uniformed men began to usher people toward the front door.

As the final members of the group went out the door, the guides in the Historical Society uniforms began telling a story of a young bride and a young slave boy, killed in the house by Confederate soldiers. The bride tried to protect the young boy from being taken from his mother during the latter days of the War Between the States. "Our lady was active today," said one of the men in uniform. "She sure put on a good show, and we get to go home early,"

FLOWER CHILDREN

In the sixties, they called us Flower Children. Hippies, Peaceniks, you've heard of us, I'm sure. Now, we're the baby boomers, the result of the big war.

Our generation involved in a piddling little war in a foreign jungle nobody ever heard of, until young boys in neighborhoods across the country got drafted to go. That didn't mean anything except a lot of body bags flying into obscure little airbases in the middle of the night. Mothers cried but Jane Fonda, more vocal, sided with the Viet Cong.

We lived in a big apartment in an old house nobody loved anymore. Mattresses lay on the floor, surrounded by ashtrays nobody bothered to pick up or empty. Other furnishings in the place included a few swayback Salvation Army sofas and some army issued body bags, stolen from the National Guard Armory, stuffed with pine straw, used them like bean bags.

My cousin and I hitchhiked cross-country from Florida to San Francisco, changing our names to Sunshine and Sweetheart Rose somewhere along the way. Our unofficial leader called herself Rose Moon. Most of us didn't use our real names; we used the names we wished for ourselves. Sunshine, Daffodil, Sweetheart Rose, more, but the names slipped away from my mind with the years.

Rose Moon kept us together; she led us into the

protests so popular back then. Most of us felt less than she for the movement. We spent our days making enough money to pay rent, eat, and buy the marijuana we smoked. She felt passionately our country was involved in a war we could not win, should not win. A no-win situation in her eyes and she led us to the marches with a Carrie Nation determination that never faltered.

We wore our hair long, most wore it straight. If not naturally straight, we ironed with a warm iron so it fell down our backs like silk ribbons. The longest hair revered and Rose Moon's blonde hair the longest and straightest.

The boys let theirs dry naturally, bushy and tangled. Grooming out of fashion for the men, and they never did. We didn't live dirty, as most people thought, just unshaven, undeodorized, unpretentious.

Rose Moon announced a big peace march on July fourth, in Washington, D. C. Those of us pregnant, she farthest along, argued against going that year, but she insisted.

Six of us, I think, or seven, doesn't really matter now, I guess, but sometimes I want to be sure to get this straight in my mind. She so enthusiastic, her enthusiasm led us beyond mundane matters of how we would travel, buy gas, or eat. To her it didn't matter, those things would take care of themselves, and in the end they did. Others of us put a little money aside for the few weeks until July, and a fellow called Beach Bum picked us up in his old

Volkswagen van.

Beach Boys and Beatles serenaded us all the way from San Francisco to Washington and we rode happy. With all windows down, we hung our heads out when the heat got too bad. Most times, the heat didn't bother us. On a mission of peace led by Rose Moon, nothing else mattered.

Rose Moon, in her advanced pregnancy, tired easily, but she smiled at us and we sang and all came right with the world. Two others of us also pregnant but Rose Moon was due first. We looked forward to the births of a new generation, a new era of peace and free love.

July fourth dawned bright and blue hot. We managed to sneak into the restroom of a corner gas station to clean up and dress, long sweeping dresses of unbleached muslin, with lace on the bodice and ruffles on the skirt. We brushed our hair till it shown and emerged ready for the big march.

We arrived at the beginning of the march at what is now the Washington Mall, more blue uniformed policemen than marchers. The hatred on their faces the same as on the National Guard faces at Kent State the following year, the same as every march we attended. They hated Peaceniks, marchers, protesters, anyone not in uniform.

We arrived early, but not long after more marchers drifted in. The excitement a little subdued until the music started, we joined hands in large groups as we started the long walk. We could walk for an hour or so.

Rose Moon began to yell at policemen. "Pigs, baby killers, rapists." Trying to make them angry.

Hatred on their faces showed us their anger from the beginning. We tried to get Rose Moon to back away from the blue uniforms, but possessed with more than anger and hatred, she stormed on. She yelled something at the policeman closest to her and chaos erupted. We never knew what caused the policeman to swing his nightstick. He hit the side of her head and she fell. He kicked her after she fell, like stepping on a roach, then walked away.

The march, over for us, we picked her up and started walking back toward the van. Our group realized as soon as we lay her down her labor had started. Rose Moon moaning and blood was everywhere.

Beach Bum drove the van to a hospital whose emergency room doctors did not want her. Crying and begging, we convinced one doctor to admit her.

Six hours later she hemorrhaged, died. The baby fine, they said. They would not release the baby to anyone except a family member. None of us even knew Rose Moon's real name. As far as we were concerned, we were her real family. We argued, but in the end,
we left the baby, the hospital, Washington, and went home.

Crossroad, Rose Moon's closest friend, told us her

pregnancy had been the result of being raped by a policeman when arrested at one of her marches back in California.

Our group broke up after that. Beach Bum's real name was Hiram. We got married three days before my baby came. Beach Bum, not his father, was always his daddy. We turned into the same conservative people as our parents.

Hiram, drafted a few months later, got both his legs blown off in that jungle. He died last year. We never had other children, but Hiram Junior was a perfect child, and we lived happy.

Hiram Junior joined the Army to be just like his patriotic daddy. This morning an Army Chaplain came to the door to tell me he was killed in a desert, on the other side of the world, nobody ever heard of until he, and so many others, chose to go.

I Do

I didn't know, the day I said I do, I wouldn't. I thought I would, really I did. Don't most of us when we say I do? How many people get married with the intention of reneging on the promise? I thought I would be married for the rest of my life.

There I was, standing in front of the dumpy little judge in a dusty little office, saying the words that would glue me to this man forever, I thought.

That man was shorter than me. The judge, I mean. Short and dumpy, he appeared more pregnant than I was, but I was barely three months along at the time. His belly stuck out like twelve months if a day. He wore a grey three piece suit made for him because no store in the world had one of those on the rack, and certainly not in those days.

We arrived at eleven o'clock and Ernie already going to miss a day's work because we had to get this done. My daddy didn't exactly threaten him with a shotgun, only because he didn't own a shotgun.

Judge Grady called his wife over from their house around the corner to be a witness along with his secretary, and we got married in just about ten minutes, from walking in to walking out. Seems it ought to take longer than that.

The judge's wife invited us over to their house to eat lunch, but Ernie said we needed to get back home. We needed to find some place to live.

We found a tiny, two bedroom, furnished house with ratty furniture, but we made the best of it until we could do better. I started saving right away for the doctor and hospital bills. I also saved for us to do better. Better seemed like a long way off, though. When you're saving from a mechanic's wages and your husband is an alcoholic, saving is almost impossible.

Three babies in three years, afraid we wouldn't make the long haul, but what could I do but hang in? First, I stopped having babies. To do that I proposed having my tubes tied, and I argued with my husband, my mother, my doctor, my preacher, for God's sake! I got my tubes tied - after one more surprise for taking so long to convince all those folks.

Fifteen years in I took on a niece and two nephews to raise, when I thought things might change for us and I could do something different. Sad story, but an accident took their parents. What else to do but take them in? Grandchildren followed; we've looked like an orphanage around here ever since.

Ernie, never a mean drunk, was a loving drinker and a philosopher. He spent a lot of time with the children, discussing their school work, their social skills, their ambitions, their futures. Did he ever give any thought to the fact I might have wished for a different future? Did he ever wish for a different future? We never talked about it.

Now, for over forty years and we're still raising children. Will it never end? Don't get me wrong, I love each and every one of them. We've raised a houseful of college graduates, a doctor, a lawyer, architect, social workers, three teachers and all kinds of computer gurus. But when do I get some time for myself?

What is it I want to do? You may well ask, but I don't know. I never had time to sit and decide what I wanted to be when I grew up. Sixteen when I married Ernie, I turned seventeen before my first child came. Married now for over forty years, I'm a great grandmother. My granddaughter recently asked me to keep her daughter while she goes to Afghanistan. Guess I'll be raising her for a while.

Oh, Ernie quit drinking yesterday; he'll never drink again. He never came to bed last night, first time in over forty years. I found him this morning in his recliner with the television still on.

GOOD LOOKING GUYS

"Well, see, Aunt Gert, I found myself married to this good looking guy. . ."

"Whoa, back up, Susie." Gert stopped her with a raised hand. "You don't just wake up one morning and find yourself married, good looking guy or not. You didn't start at the beginning of this story like I told you. Now go back and start over."

"Well, Aunt Gert, we ran into these good looking guys down at Bubba Jack's place down at the Ogeechee River. That juke joint he has a couple of miles from town? He's got a bar and a couple of houseboats down there for folks to sleep in if they get too drunk to drive home."

"I'll bet that's what they're used for," Gert snorted.

"Damn, Aunt Gert. Do you want me to finish this story or not?"

"Don't be cussing around me. How many times I got to tell you?" Gert raised her hand like she was going to slap her.

Susie threw her hands up in surrender. "I'm sorry, Aunt Gert, I forgot."

"Don't be forgetting any more, if you know what's good for you. Now tell me this story or get out of my house."

"Yes ma'am, see, we met them one night when we

35

went out to Bubba Jack's down on the river. You remember that place has a band on Friday and Saturday nights? Well, me and Janine and Lucy got Judd to drive us out there, and we went to hear this new band. Now I know what you always told me about staying away from the good looking guys, Aunt Gert, but this one guy kept looking at me. And I kept looking at him."

"Now, I can tell there's a lot more to this story than a proposal, and you finding yourself married," Gert said, leaning back in her chair. "Don't leave out any details. Go on, girl."

"Well, Aunt Gert, I'm plum ashamed to tell you the next part, but I found myself in one of those beds in one of those houseboats the next morning. But I don't remember how I got there."

"Were you naked?"

"No!" Susie's face turned red. "I had all my clothes on and he did, too."

"Is that when he asked you to marry him?" Gert stood, refilled her coffee cup, and sat

again in record speed, ready for the rest of the story.

"No, ma'am, but he did want to meet me at Bubba Jack's again, so I said yes. Well, Janine and Lucy and me, we got done up and went again. He was there all right, but when I walked in, he's dancing with some other girl. It's okay, though, 'cause when that dance got over, he come over and sat down

36

beside me. He brought a couple of friends with him and they come over, too."

"Is this story gonna drag on with y'all meeting these guys night after night?" Gert asked, putting a little boredom in her voice.

"Oh no, Aunt Gert, now's when it starts getting good. Janine and Lucy and me, we didn't drink any. One of those guys goes up to get us some drinks at the bar. When he handed them, I passed mine off to Judd. This good looking guy didn't like it none, but I told him I owed Judd a drink and paying off the favor. Well, he got pissed off, but what could he do?"

"Go on, get to the getting married part." Gert anxious for the rest of the story.

"So, of course, the girls knew not to drink the stuff they brought us, but we sat and nursed our drinks, pretending. This good looking guy started asking me to marry him, and he was good looking enough. I might'a considered it, if I hadn't already been married to my Judd."

Gert laughed out loud. "Yeah, like you and Judd ain't joined at the hip. Now, tell me where was Judd all the time this waking up in that man's bed was going on?"

"Judd was watching over me the whole time. He's the one got the guy so drunk he couldn't walk. But Judd was watching me all night. You know how he is. Now all three of those guys are going to jail for possession of that date rape drug and a whole lot of others Judd found in their car. They're wanted from here all the way back to California. Judd says the three of us are the best deputies he has. I truly bless the day I found myself married to that good looking rascal you raised."

LUCY

Lucy stood, looking out the window, holding a coffee mug in both hands. The feel of him coming into the room, she steeled her body not to flinch as he put his hands on her shoulders.

He felt her tension because he demanded, "You know I'm sorry, don't you?"

"Yes, Lester, you're always sorry," she whispered in her softest voice.

Coffee flew from the cup, as he snatched her around, and splashed down the front of his white shirt.

The mug bounced on the carpet and shattered on the fireplace hearth a few feet away.

The fury on his face no longer frightened her after so many years. She stood before him, flinched, but unmoving, knowing to run would increase his wrath.

"Why do you make me do this, Lucy?" he screeched in her face. Old cigarette smoke on his breath made her want to gag, and tiny droplets of spittle peppered her face.
Hands circled her throat before she could move, and she stood, waiting. Shaking, backward, forward, over and over, her teeth coming together and her mouth opening and closing, over and over.

Closing her eyes as she saw his fist coming, no

chance to duck, ducking would make it worse. She rolled with his punch, falling to the floor with her back to him. It hurt less when he kicked her back than front. Drawing her arms under, she waited for the kicking to stop, refusing to give in and scream. Tears streamed down her cheeks. Oh, yes, tears flowed. She never learned to stop the tears, but he taught her to stop the screams.

A replay of the previous evening, he soon tired of beating. He turned and walked away as though tired of the game. She lay, taking inventory. Only bruises, or broken bones again this time? The familiar sounds of his taking off the spoiled shirt, changing clothes in the bedroom, told her he may be leaving soon. She waited.

"Get up and clean up that mess you made," he shouted as he walked out the door.

She waited until sure he was gone before attempting to rise. She swept up the shattered coffee mug, blotted up the spilled coffee and did her best to remove the stain from the carpet.

Lucy took a couple of aspirin, poured herself another mug of coffee, and went to stand by the window.

THE ORANGE TABBY

Groans and chugging of a smoke stack broke the silence. Soon the roar of the eighteen wheeler straining up the hill to our house drowned out all other sound for Tabby and me. When the brakes squealed, I stood in the kitchen doorway watching Tabby's arched back. She hissed, and sprang down the unstable steps of the porch when she felt thunder from the truck straining up the long driveway into the muddy yard. Refusing to show Clyde her fear, she scampered away before he stumbled from the truck.

Tabby scrambled to a place behind the chimney to attend her two remaining kittens. A couple of weeks before, I watched as she managed to spirit those away before Clyde found the others in the back yard shed and stomped them to death. He would not find these; the children assured the tabby. My children talked to her as though she understood them. They crawled under the house to her and the kittens. His big, paunchy belly would never be able to crawl under the house.

Clyde nearly fell out of the truck. He's drunk again. I turned to shoo the children to their room, but they were nowhere in sight. They figured it out before I did, or maybe they just took precautions. I hurried to the kitchen, knowing to have a plate waiting for him when he got in, I set a glass of iced tea beside his plate when he came into the kitchen. I sat down across the table, waiting for him to speak.

"What you been doing all day?" he demanded. His eyes blood-shot, he hadn't bathed or shaved in a couple of days.

"We walked to town, bought some groceries, and cooked supper. It's been raining all week," I said in a voice I hated, begging him not to start on me tonight.

"How'd you get to the store?"

"We walked, like we always do."

"How much'd you spend?"

"About thirty dollars, like you told me, Clyde."

"Give me the slip."

I pulled the charge slip from my purse, handing it to him reluctantly.

"This says thirty three dollars and ninety five cents."

"I'm sorry. Try to understand, everything is more expensive at George's than at the supermarket in Thomaston."

"When I say thirty dollars, I mean thirty dollars, not a penny more." He finished his meal, looking at me across the table, waiting for me to argue or whine.

"Clyde, I can't feed five children and us on thirty dollars a week, no matter how much beans and cornbread we eat. Children need fruits and

42

vegetables."

He moved so fast I didn't see his fist coming at me. How can a man so big move so fast? I found myself on the floor, overturned chair and all. He snatched the chair away, and his boot kicked my backside, up and down my hip and legs. I didn't scream or cry very loud, made him worse, and might make the children come out to help. That would be the worst thing.

***

We met when Clyde was a senior in high school, and I only fourteen, a freshman. Right away he decided he wanted me. Over

the years I figured it was because he wanted a woman who wouldn't talk back. My daddy liked Clyde from the start. He told Mama it would be good to have a son-in-law who worked and had money to loan. Clyde had a job waiting for him as soon as he graduated and a regular income for Daddy to borrow. A joke Clyde saw through right away.

Not called date rape back then, but it happened all the same. Clyde forced himself on me the second time we ever went off together. Went off - not out. Never a real date like movies or out to eat, we went to ride in his pride and joy, an old car he fixed up himself. He'd buy me a Coke, but never anything to eat. We never went where the other kids went or hung out. After that second ride, we never went anywhere except to park in a lane behind the old cemetery.

Clyde did let me go to his high school graduation, but afterward went off with a bunch of pals, and I walked home. Daddy found out about my pregnancy, and he went to confront Clyde. By that time, Clyde was nineteen and I was still fourteen.

We got married three days after graduation and six months before Clyde Junior came. C. J. weighed nine pounds. The doctor warned us to wait six weeks before 'resuming sexual relations' but Clyde didn't believe in waiting for anything. Bertha, named for his grandma, came nine and a half months later.

The only thing I did was make babies and take care of them. 1 learned pretty fast. Over the next few years I did a lot of both. Clyde knocked me around the few times I talked about getting a job.

He was on the road driving a truck most weeks. Way back in the beginning he called home two or three times a day. He always called collect and asked for himself.

He'd give me exactly the amount to spend on groceries, bring a

receipt and the change back to him.
Clyde grumbled real bad when C. J. started school and needed money for things. The school or PTA asked the students to sell magazine subscriptions or wrapping paper to raise money for things the school board couldn't buy. C. J. needed new crayons, or a writing tablet, things the school didn't supply. He called the teachers and the school to complain.

After a while, the teachers stopped asking for money, or supplies.

If the children got sick and I took them to the doctor, he slapped me around and accused me of babying them when the bills came. The doctor saw my face and stopped sending bills.

Clyde drove a truck long distance. I guess if he hadn't been gone so much, I'd have more than five babies. By the time C. J. turned six, Bertha was five. Hector, three (named for Clyde's daddy,) Agnes, two, (named for Clyde's mama,) and Grady, one, (named for Clyde's Mama's maiden name,) one by one they came, and I loved them all . He kicked me hard enough to lose a couple of babies along the way, one since Grady was born, a year before. I grieved for my lost babies, but Clyde never showed any grief. That early along, I didn't even go to the hospital, no one to keep the children.

With Clyde on the road, gone, the kids and I got along fine. We walked to town on Mondays, if the weather cooperated, Monday being the only day he would let me leave the house. Besides the grocery store, we went to the library and got enough books for me to read to them all week. We settled into a routine that worked for us, and every day we planned things to do.

Clyde's Mama gave me an old wringer washing machine when she got her new automatic. Tuesdays I washed clothes and hung them on the lines to dry. We straightened up the house. I played games with the little ones not in school learning colors, shapes, things I read they needed to know.

Wednesdays I ironed most all day, Clyde's shirts like he wanted them by the time he got home, when he came home at all. Before little Grady came, Clyde quit coming home much anymore. His mama came to stay with the other children for the two days I spent in the hospital and left as soon as I came home.

He left a credit with Mr. George down at the store and he kept paying, because Mr. George didn't stop me from getting groceries. I got real good at making do with a little money, lots better than those fancy magazine stories I read in the doctor's office.

On Thursday and Friday I spent those days cleaning the house and getting ready for

Clyde to come home on Friday night, if he came home. I never knew whether to plan for

him or not, didn't care. We enjoyed our life when Clyde was on the road.

***

This time he was drunk and in a bad temper. I hoped the children would stay in their room, away from their daddy. If I stayed quiet enough, maybe they would. After all the kicking and hitting, the pain too much for me to be quiet any longer, and I started crying.

Clyde glanced around at C. J. and Bertha peaking out the door of their room and started yelling at them to go to bed. Only about seven thirty, poor little C. J. tried to argue they stayed up later on weekends.

I went into their room and thought I quieted them when Clyde yelled, "If y'all don't shut up, I'll give you something to cry about."

I kissed my babies and got them quiet, knowing I needed to get out before Clyde came in.

While I was taking his dirty clothes out of a fancy new suitcase to wash them the next week, he started on the kids again. I went to find out what was going on. He only hit me a few more times, but by morning my face swelled and my eyes would barely open.

Before he even got out of bed the next morning, Clyde said, "Wash all those clothes I brought yesterday. I need them next week."

"I already packed your suitcase with the ones I washed and ironed last week," I said, getting out of bed.

"I said wash the rest of them today."

"Okay, soon as breakfast is over." No point in arguing with him, I'd do it anyway.

After rain most all week, I hung clothes on the sagging lines, hoping they would dry before rain started again. I noticed Hector with his Daddy's old screwdriver playing around the tire on the off side of Clyde's big truck. Tires not much good anyway, I let him play. Clyde was taking a nap, and I wanted to keep the kids quiet. I walked around the truck to check on Hector. Digging a hole beside the big truck's front tire, he handed me the screwdriver when I asked. Using the long tool, I played around, checking the depth of the tread on the tires.

Tabby came under the truck, rubbed her head on me, and stood inside, beside the big tire.

"What's it you see, Tabby?" I whispered, watching as she stood looking at the tire beside her, moving so I could tell what she studied. A cut. Looking closer it might be all the way through, or close enough as to be . . . easy to cause a slow leak. I stomped mud back in the hole Hector made and told him to dig over at the truck's back side.

Clothes were dry and in a basket when Clyde stepped out the front door. Seeing Hector walk around the front of the truck with the old screwdriver, he dove down the steps, snatched the screwdriver away from my boy, and backhanded him into a patch of mud.

The basket fell and clothes spilled as I rushed to Hector. Clyde caught me, he slapped me and began hitting me with his fists. I knew what was coming and fighting would make it worse. The kids ran into the house and hid in their room.

When Clyde got mad, he took it out on anyone who got in his way, or anyone he saw, so I taught them to get out of sight. Hector still cried while Clyde hit me and knocked me down. I started crying and screaming so he wouldn't hear the kids crying. It made him madder, kicking me and snatching me up by my hair.

He finished with me and stormed into the house. I ran after him, all set to kill him if he laid a hand on my children. He headed into our bedroom, grabbed his suitcase, and started back out the door.

He turned and said, "I ain't coming back. I found a woman who wants me around. She don't have any squalling brats to interfere with my rest and relaxing." I stood, stared at him, wanted to say fine with me, and I didn't care.

The sun setting, he started up the big eighteen-wheeler, as rain started. The roads would be slick.

Clyde gone, the kids came from their bedroom where they hid and gathered around while I washed my face with a cool cloth. They started crying when they saw me. My eyes swollen almost closed again and I couldn't sit comfortably.

"How'd you manage to keep Grady quiet?" I asked C. J. My six-year-old usually managed to pull off a miracle when Clyde came home, and I always showed him my appreciation.

"Like you do, Mama. I held him, and rocked him. I fixed him a bottle when I could get to the kitchen," C. J. answered. Tears welled in his eyes, and my heart felt broken for all my children. My fault they went through this so many times. But what could I do, and where could I take them?

The kids calmed down, and I lay on the couch resting with all of them huddled around, when the sheriff showed up. I never called him in all the years Clyde and I were together, it would have made things worse.

"Mrs. Hanner, are you all right?" he asked me before anything else when he saw my face.
I assured him I was, asked him to call me Jeanne, even told him this was nothing new.

He came to tell me Clyde's truck, going 'hellbent for leather' downhill from the house, had gone off the road, down the only steep hill in the county. Seems the truck skidded on the wet road.

"He may've had a blowout that caused the wreck," he said. The truck burst into flames at the bottom with Clyde trapped inside. Some people heard him screaming and tried to get him out, but the door jammed. By the time the fire department got there, it was too late to get him out alive. "I sure am sorry to tell you this, Mrs. Hanner. Seems like there wasn't nothing to be done for him."
I pulled Agnes and Grady up in my lap and buried my face in their hair, trying to dredge up a tear or two, but couldn't.

"We need to take you to the hospital, let them check you out. Looks like you've been in a wreck yourself. Did Clyde do this to you? Why didn't you ever call us?"

"I'm fine sheriff," I said, over and over, finally convincing him. "Been hurt worse than this before."

I didn't even call my parents. They didn't speak to me anymore since Clyde laughed at them when they asked for money.

About time I started to go to bed, Clyde's Mama came knocking on the door, with a suitcase in her hand. Who the hell called you? I wondered.

"I come to stay with you to help with the arrangements and keep them kids in line for you," she said. I stood for a while looking at her.

"I don't need you here," I said. No more mealy mouth for me. That felt good. "You can meet me at the funeral home tomorrow, if you want to, and you can go to the funeral, if you want to. You can't stay here."

"How dare you talk to me like that!" she huffed, and reached for the handle on the screen

door. I latched the door and told her to go. "I'm tired, and I need some rest, and we don't need you here."
Without acknowledging the bruises on my face, she glared at me with hatred, not the first time, turned and huffed away, mumbling something I didn't catch and didn't care about anyway.

Next day, the sheriff's wife came to pick us up and take us to the funeral home to make the arrangements. Clyde's Mama already there, decided everything, I didn't care. If it made her feel better to be in charge, so be it. The woman planned the funeral for the next

day so she wouldn't be extra days at a motel.

Not many people at the funeral, Clyde so mean he didn't have many friends. I didn't either, but I seemed to be making some new friends, the sheriff, his wife.

Two cheap looking women showed up, but I didn't care. Their makeup looked to be applied with a trowel, earrings hanging to their fake boobs, skirts so tight they could barely sit. What difference would it make? Soon over and Marla, the sheriff's wife, took me and my kids home. I guess I appeared a sight with bruises all over and my eyes still barely open. Nobody even asked about my bruises or said much. I couldn't cry, but his mama put on a show.

Next day, a social worker from the welfare department came to take us to town to apply for Clyde's Social Security for me and the kids.

His boss called to say he'd send me a check for Clyde's life insurance. I never knew there was so much money in the world.

Mr. Chester told me, "When Clyde first started working, he wanted to put his mama on the policy. But I told him it was necessary to put a wife on if he was married. That's not absolutely true, but you and these kids need this money a lot more than his mama."

For the first time in days, a small smile came to my face. "Thanks, Mr. Chester. That's the nicest thing anybody's ever done for me."

I put the insurance money in the bank. We live real good on the Social Security. The insurance and the interest goes in a savings account for my children so they can go to college. I bought us a car, and the sheriff sent a deputy to teach me how to drive. The kids and I still go to town on Monday.

Now I can pay the doctor and drugstore when we get sick. I pay for groceries when I buy them and buy the kids clothes when they need them.

Tabby and her two kittens got fixed and they have the run of the place now. The kids love

them, chasing them up and down the steps on our new porch.

One of Clyde's old 'friends' showed up one day asking if I'd like some 'company.'

I told him, "No, but those floozies that showed up at his funeral might. Why don't you go hunt them up?"

AIR CASTLES

The first time Jim and I played 'show me yours and I'll show you mine,' we turned eleven and there wasn't much to show. Fun, and we planned to get married when we graduated from college but before he went to medical school.

We had early lunch period, and recess during lunch period, so, if you went to early lunch, you got the longest recess period, too.

Jim knew about this storage closet in the gym that was never locked. We went in there and Jim took my t-shirt off and he took off his t-shirt and we looked at our chests. Well, my chest was as flat as his. What the hell?

He told me that day, "I knew yours would be pretty much like mine, your shirt didn't poke out. But let's keep watching like this and we'll watch your progress over the years, okay?"

He put his finger on my flat nipple and rubbed a little, and it felt good, so I did the same thing to him. We smiled because it felt good to him, too.

He leaned over and put his mouth on my flat nipple and licked with his tongue. Wow, did that feel good! So, I did the same to him. When he put his hand on his pants, I asked what he was doing.

"It's hard."

"What's hard?" Now, I had seen a penis before,

really. A boy baby. His only got hard when he had to pee, so I asked Jim if he had to pee.

"No, I think it's hard because we've been playing around."

"Oh." I didn't know what else to say. What can you say? "Can I see?"

"Not this time," he said, and tried to push it down. Maybe he tried to keep it from being hard. Maybe he did need to pee.

"Okay," I said. "Can I touch, like this?" I reached out and touched it through his clothes, but he groaned and fell back.

"No!" he said, and pushed my hand away. Was he mad? Then I saw. It looked like he peed a little in his pants, a wet spot on the front.

"Why'd you do that?" he asked, acting mad at me.

I couldn't help myself, I started crying. I started looking for my t-shirt and put it on. When I stood to leave, he grabbed my hand and pulled me down again.

"Wait, Audrey," he begged. "Please don't go."

I still cried and couldn't stop. He held my hand, put his arm around my shoulder, and pulled me close like always when nobody would see.

"That's what happens when a man does it to a woman," he said.

"Does what?"

"You know, sex."

"We didn't do sex, did we?"

"No, we didn't, but when it gets hard like that, and the man has sex, it spits out stuff."

"Even with his clothes on?"

"Well, usually he takes his clothes off, I think."

"I don't think we know enough about this to try again, do you?"

"Maybe you're right," he said, like he didn't believe me. "I need to go put on my gym shorts."

So, that's the first time we played the game, but not the last. We got better.

I found these books in my mama's closet, a big stack of books hidden under some old clothes. I only took two of them.

She'll never miss them. She probably had a dozen or more and I can't imagine her and my daddy ever had any use for them.

YOUR DADDY

CHAPTER 1

"Your daddy walked off and left us and all the other women whats pregnant by him," Jamaria screamed, anger and frustration evident. "Didn't you know? He left all of us. You, me, and all these other womens, too."

"Not my daddy," Kacy cried. "He wouldn't do that." She crumpled into the grass beside the road and sobbed into the tail of her ragged dress.

She sat beside the crying girl and tried to put an arm around her. The girl drew away and scrambled out of reach. Kacy was only five, how could she be expected to understand?

Jamaria sat without speaking until the sobs subsided, moved over enough to put a hand on the crying girl's back.

"Listen to me, Kacy. Your daddy's a good man, in his way. But he's a rounder. He liked the women and they liked him. All us women did. Now they's three of us gonna bear his babies and he's gone from these parts. Now I don't 'spect he'll be gone long, but right now he's gone and he left you with me. I don't understand why he chose me to take care of you, but we stuck with each other for a while."

"How long's he gonna be gone?" Kacy asked, looking at Jamaria for the first time since she crumpled.

"Well, girl, he didn't tell me, he left me a little money to look after you and me and said he'd be back sometime."

Kacy stared at Jamaria, wiped tears from her face with the hem of her dress and stood. "If my daddy left some money for us, can I get a new school dress?"

"I think we can arrange that." They walked down the dusty road to the four room house at the next intersection.

Over fried chicken and mashed potatoes later, Kacy asked, "Did my daddy leave me with you 'cause we was at your house when he decided to leave?"

"No, I think he made arrangements to be here when he decided to leave. Do you see the difference?" Kacy nodded, started to speak, but didn't.

Washing dishes together, Kacy started again to say something, but didn't.

Sitting in the bathtub, Kacy called Jamaria into the bathroom. "This is a mighty nice place to live, ain't it?"

"Well, I'm mighty glad to live here. My mama died and left this house to me, used to belong to my granny before she died. Needs some work, but it belong to me now. I don't owe nothing."

"We can paint, if you wanted to change the colors."

"More coats of paint to cover these old boards than my arms can do after I work all day, but we might tackle it after the baby comes. Maybe we can do that befo' I to go back to work after the baby's born."

"When the baby coming?"

"I've still got almost six months to go, a long time and through the hot summer."

"Where the baby gonna sleep?"

"Since your daddy is gone, I guess I'll put him in my room."

"We can put her in my room, I can help you take care of it. What you want anyway, a girl or a boy?"

"I don't know. Do all little girls ask as many questions as you do?" They laughed together.

"Problly not, but little boys like to play with snakes and frogs."

"Ewww," they both said, and laughed together again.

Jamaria sat on the bed beside Kacy as she put her to bed. She caressed her hair, held her hand and whispered, "Your daddy loves you. He'll be back, don't worry."

Kacy's tears welled and she sniffed. "I don't know if he'll ever come back."

"Why do you say that?"

"He never left me before. I'm scared."

"He be back, baby, your daddy love you."

"I sure hope so." Kacy turned her back to Jamaria so her tears couldn't be seen and cried herself to sleep.

Jamaria woke Kacy in time for school the next morning, and they ate breakfast.

"My head hurts a little," Kacy said as they left for school.

"That's problly 'cause you cried yourself to sleep last night. My head hurts in the morning when I do. If your head don't get better, git them to call me at work."

"Really?"

"Sure, baby, it's what they do, ain't it?"

"Like you my mama?"

"Well, yeah, I guess." Jamaria surprised at the expression on Kacy's face.

Kacy ran to Jamarie's house from the school bus stop and stormed in the door. "Is my daddy home yet?"

"No, but, honey, we can't 'spect him to be back this

soon. He only left yeste'day. I'm 'specting him to be gone for months. He probly won't be back before this baby gets born."

"He never left me this long afore. Why would he go off and leave me here with somebody I don't even know?" She burst into tears and threw herself on the couch.

"He's a man, honey. Ain't no 'splaining why a man does anything." Jamaria moved to the couch and put her hand on Kacy's back, rubbing up and down. "Now you jest get up and come in the kitchen. Let's get you a cold drink and a snack. Gonna be a while before supper. My frien' Rosanna comin' to eat with us and she don't get off work 'til seven."

Kacy sat up suddenly. "Why you home? I thought you didn't get off 'til after five."

"I thought I might need to be here for you today. This is your first day coming home to my house. Tomorrow I get off work at five, but you can come up to the store, if you want to."

"Yeah, I don't think I wanna be here by myself."

"That's what I thought." Jamarie patted Kacy's back and led her into the kitchen. "You can do your homework after your snack."

Kacy laughed. "We don't get homework in kindygarden."

"You don't? Well, you can color me a pi'ture."

Rosanna examined Kacy, getting her measure. "Girl, you don't look nothing like your daddy."

"Hush," Jamaria said from beside the stove. She turned to frown at Rosanna and waved her words away.

"He always say I jes' like my mama," Kacy said, watching Jamaria open a can with the electric opener.

"What'cha doing?" she asked.

"I'm making sammon croquets," she answered. "Watch, I drain the sammon, I pick the bones and skin away. Fork the meat to mix with onion and cornmeal and eggs. I patty them up in little round cakes." She demonstrated as she went along, stopping long enough to stir a pot of cheese grits and turn the burner off. "I'm gonna fry up these things in the grease and they gonna be good with these cheese grits and peas. If you eat all your supper, you get dessert. I brought a lemon pie home from the store. Set the table, this'll be ready in a few minutes."

Rosanna handed her the plates from a cabinet Kacy couldn't reach. The girl put a fork in each plate and a glass of iced tea above. She sat down at the side of the table waiting for supper. "Glad I ate a snack when I got home from school, 'cause I'm starving again now."

"You would be, growing young'un's always hungry."

64

Jamaria put the last of the food on the table and the three of them held hands around the table. "Bless this food, oh Lord, we pray. Keep us safe by night and day. Amen." Jamaria and Rosanna each squeezed Kacy's hands.

"Why you squeezed my hands?"

"That's to say we love you," Rosanna said. "We always do at my daddy and mama's house every meal. We still do when I eat with them."

"How can you say you love me? I only just met you right now."

"Jesus loves everybody and we s'posed to love everybody, too. That's how we love you."

"Am I s'posed to love you, too?"

"If you love Jesus, you are."

"Well, I been told about Jesus, but I don't know as I love him."
"How 'bout I take you with me to church on Sunday? You can learn more 'bout him and decide for yo'self. You want to go, Jamaria?"

"I got to work Sunday, but Kacy can go, if she want."

"Yeah, I wanna go," the girl said, jumping in her chair.

"Okay, I pick you up before Jamaria go to work.

Now eat yo supper."

"Are you one of them ladies having babies for my daddy?"

"Lord, no, chile." Rosanna said, and Jamaria sputtered while they laughed, looking at each other.

Jamaria and Rosanna sat in the small, clean, sparsely furnished living room after Kacy went to bed. They shared a beer, something that wasn't good for the pregnant woman, figuring half wouldn't hurt.

"How long you gonna try and keep the girl?" Rosanna asked, looking over the rim of her glass.

"She's staying with me 'til Montre comes back."

"What kind of name is that? What if he don't come back?"

"He told me his mama read a lot. If he don't come back, she'll stay with me."

"You can't afford to keep her. How you gone raise two young'uns?"

"Lots of womens do. I can, too." she said, lowering her voice and looking toward the room where Kacy slept. "He told me she ain't even his girl. He took up with her mama when she a baby. Her mama took off when she 'bout two. He been raisin' her ever since. He might not come back. Somebody's got to take care of the girl. Better me than some other folks."

"Yeah, that's right. I shore don't envy you none, though."

"She's a good girl and be a lot of help to me with the baby."

Rosanna rose to leave; at nearly six feet, she towered over Jamaria, only five feet two.

Rosanna Franklin's features uneven, skin the color of milk chocolate, eyes muddy brown, never described as even passably handsome, presented as a leader among her people in church and her profession as Licensed Practical Nurse at the local nursing home.

Her husband of one year killed years before by an accidental fall into the swamp near the farm of his father-in-law, after the old man found bruises and swollen eyes on his only daughter. The alligators got to him before the men could get a boat in the water.

At forty, she held no illusions about men, having seen too many women led astray by men who didn't stay around long enough to raise children, help financially, or even give a child his name.

Jamaria Williston, petite, thin, looks of a china doll. Her features even, skin the color of light coffee, eyes beautiful, deep brown with flecks of gold, her demeanor of an older woman than her age. A ready smile drew people. She didn't recognize her beauty or sexuality, which especially drew men. They wanted to protect her; they wanted to possess her. At thirty three, surprised at her attraction to a man as handsome as Montre Desmonte. Now, paying the price for that attachment. Love or lust, didn't matter, amounted to the same thing. She still paid a cost.

Before locking the door, she waved as Rosanna drove away. She leaned against the door, rubbed her arms, squeezed them around her waist. Help us, dear Lord.

She stopped by Kacy's room to check on her, pulled the covers up, patted her back, and went to her own bedroom. The child, small for five, dragged around with Montre for years while he went from low paid job to lower paid job, from one available woman to the next. Montre always found a woman everywhere he went to take care of him and the girl, she the most recent in a long line of gullible women.

Jamaria talked big to her friend, but dealing with and taking care of a five year old, not her child, and a new baby? Always biting off more than I can chew. She covered her hair and got a quick shower, knowing there would be no time in the morning.

"Wake up, sweet girl," Jamaria crooned next morning. "I'm taking you to school today and make arrangements for you to ride the bus to my job."

"You gone take me? I ain't ridin' the bus?"

"You gonna ride the bus tomorrow, but today I want to get things straight with the school."

"Awright, what's fo breakfast?"

"Left over cheese grits and toast. Now git up and wash yo face."

**

"Good mornin', Miss Mildred," Jamaria said to the lady behind a counter at the school. "I can't believe you still running this place. Seems like you been here since the beginning of time." The women laughed together, made small talk for a moment.

"Kacy is gonna be staying with me for a while and I need to make sure things are all right

here at school. I have a letter here from her daddy."

"Let me see, Jamaria. I probably need to get a copy for our records." Mildred Peterson took the letter, read it over twice and regarded at Jamaria. "Is he coming back for her?" she asked, in a lowered voice.

Jamaria glanced at Kacy sitting in a chair behind her. "Okay if she goes on to her class? I want to make sure she can ride a bus to the IGA store this afternoon and every day but Tuesday. I'm off on Tuesday. If I'm off another day, I'll pick her up."

"Yeah, I think we can. Kacy, honey, why don't you go on to your class. I think the bus you ride to the store will be number seventeen. Do you know what seventeen looks like?"

"Yes, ma'am. A one and a seven."

"That's right. When the bell rings this afternoon,

you go get on the bus and get off at Jamaria's store. The bus driver will tell you where."

Kacy looked at Jamaria with a fear in her eyes not seen since the first few moments of being told about her daddy. "You gone be there, ain't you?"

Jamaria knelt and hugged the girl. "I promise you I will be. You get off the bus, honey."

"Okay." The girl skipped off to class without looking back.

Jamaria leaned over the counter, and whispered, "The son of a bitch left without even sayin' goodbye to her."

"Do you think he's coming back?"

Jamaria shook her head. "He left the letter. He may be back and he may not. I'm not countin' on him."

"Whatcha gonna do with her?"

"I'm gonna keep her. Whatcha think? She needs somebody she can trust. She shore don't

need to grow up thinking every body in her life is gonna throw her away. Her mama already done that. Now her daddy?"

"I see what you mean. What if he comes back?"

"Well, we gonna talk a long time 'bout this child and the one I'm having, too. He ain't gonna haul her off again and leave her with some other woman like he did with me. He can leave her with me." She paused. "I don't really think his sorry soul's comin' back,

though. But I need to get on to work. Thanks for helping me. I need to keep the letter if I need to take Kacy to the doctor or somethin'."

"Yeah, okay, let me get a copy for our records. I'll be right back."

Jamaria sat, waiting for the letter, thinking about Montre Desmonte. The finest looking, and smoothest talking, man she ever met. When will I learn to leave the good lookin' ones alone? Ain't nothing but trouble. Although truth be told, she had only fallen for two men in her life. The first right out of high school, but luckily she didn't get as involved with Joey Tucker as with this fool she may be dealing with for a long time, or not.

"Here you go, Jamaria," Mildred said, handing the letter to her in an envelope. "I'm glad the child has someone like you taking care of her. She's such a sweet little thing. We'll do all we can to help. Y'all gone be at church on Sunday?"

"Oh, I'll be working Sunday. But Rosanna's picking Kacy up for Sunday School, keeping her all day."

Sunday morning dawned bright and cold. Jamaria turned the heat off the day before thinking it too late for this kind of cold in south Georgia. "We're going to start watching the weather," she told Kacy. They put on socks and wrapped themselves in the woman's only heavy bathrobes until the inadequate heater warmed the tiny house.

"Watching the weather? What do you mean?"

"The Weather Channel on TV."

"You got a TV? A whole channel only shows the weather?"

"Yes, in the bedroom. Maybe we need to bring it out to the living room. It ain't even been turned on since you got here. I don't watch much anyway, only get the basic channels, been thinking 'bout cancelling the whole thing."

"Can I watch cartoons?"

"Not today, we have a full day today. Rosanna will be here in a little while to get you for church. We need to get you all pretty in your new dress and shoes. I need to work."

"She's here," Kacy yelled, jumping up from the couch after breakfast. She skipped across the floor and pulled the door open. "Hey, Rosanna. Do you like my new dress?"

"Miss Rosanna," Jamaria corrected.

"Miss Rosanna, do you like my dress?"

"I do. Very much. You're beautiful in that color. Is blue your favorite color?"

"My favorite color is red, but I didn't want to buy a red dress to grow into, so we bought this blue one,

72

and now I think blue might be my next favorite color," she said, twirling, showing the dress to the tall woman. "I don't think I ever got a real new dress before."

"Well, it certainly is a pretty dress. Come over here and sit down 'fore you make yo'self dizzy."

Jamaria came from her bedroom, holding her purse and car keys in her hand. "I need to go, Kacy. You be good for Miss Rosanna today." Looking toward the tall woman she asked, "You sure you don't mind watching her for me?"

"This will be a fun day. We eating at church and singing most of the day. This girl gone get a belly full of Jesus today." Her laughter bounced around the walls of the tiny house, and Kacy giggled along with her.

Jamaria laughed, as she ushered them out the door. Sooner than Jamaria anticipated, they settled into a routine which appealed to them both. Kacy rode her bus to the IGA store where she got a small snack; Jamaria kept the receipt showing she paid. Kacy drew pictures and colored them, or practiced writing, in the break room until Jamaria got off each day.

They went home where they made supper together, they got baths and soon went to bed. Little time for TV and it still didn't get moved into the living room. Occasionally they watched for a few minutes from Jamaria's bed, checking the weather, or laughing at a cartoon.

Spring brought warmer weather and longer days; they spent most afternoons outside on

the small porch, rocking in mismatched chairs. They talked about the coming baby, what they needed to get for the baby, whether it would be a girl or boy. They seldom talked about Kacy's daddy.

Rosanna came often for supper, many times bringing covered dishes made by her mother or a sister-in-law. Sometimes she brought things for the baby, or dresses for Kacy given to her by the sisters-in-law, outgrown by their children.

One night, after they Kacy went to bed, Rosanna asked, "Whatcha gonna do with Kacy when school's out? She can't stay at the store with you."

"I shore can't afford to pay nobody."

"Mama say she keep her for you. What's one more 'mong all the grands she keep every day?" Rosanna laughed.

"I can't ask her."

"You ain't asking. She telling you," Rosanna said. "Gone keep your baby, too, she say."

"I can't afford to pay."

"It would make her mad if you offer her money. You jes like her own youngun."

Jamaria wiped at the tears spilling from her eyes and turned her head.

"Don't try to hide from me." Rosanna handed her a paper towel from the counter. "I know you and your heart, girl, how you feel 'bout my mama and how she feel 'bout you. You the closest thing I've got to a sister and you my mama's other daughter. She like you better than any of them wives my brothers brought home. She use' to ask them why they didn't marry you. They said it'd be like marrying a sister."

They laughed.

"Yeah, it'd be like me marrying a brother, too."

"Come on out Saturday night and eat supper with us, talk to Mama. She'll tell you about keeping Kacy and the baby."

"How can I thank her. I'd be embarrassed, shamed.'

"You don't never have to be shamed in front of Mama. She love you, girl."

"I love her, too. That why I be shamed."

"Hush now. Come on out Saturday night."

"Okay, Kacy'd love to spend time with all them young'uns."

"They can't wait to meet her, too."

CHAPTER 2

"Where we going?" Kacy asked when Jamaria didn't turn at her usual place on Saturday afternoon after work.

"I told you, we going to eat supper with Rosanna's mama. Don't you remember?"

"Yeah." Kacy drew the word out. "I don' know any of them people."

"You know Rosanna."

"She gone be there?" Kacy asked, looking out the window.

"Shore, she like my sister. Her mama like a mama to me, too."

"Where yo mama?"

"She died a long time ago. Mama Rosie was all I had for a while."

"Mama Rosie?"

"Rosanna's mama."

"Like you my Mama Jamaria?"

"I guess." Jamaria paused. "Yeah, jes like that."

"How far we going?"

"Not far, jes down the road a piece."

"Why we ain't been before?"

"I'll tell you sometime."

They rode in silence for the remaining few minutes, turning into the long driveway riding alongside the tall chain link fence, beside the swampy pond with large cypress trees drooping Spanish moss, toward the house at the lane's end.

Rosanna and a host of children came out to meet Jamaria's car as she parked beside the end one. The yard resembled a used car lot.

"Come on, girl, the whole crowd is waiting for you." Rosanna opened the door for Kacy.

"For me?"

"Yeah, they want to meet this pretty little girl I been talkin' 'bout."

Kacy jumped out of the car and took Rosanna's hand. Jamaria took covered dishes from the back seat. Older children came to help, everyone talked at once heading toward the kitchen entrance.

"Lawd, girl, ain't you a sight for sore eyes," Rosie Franklin called from the stove. "Come on in and let me look at you, Jamaria." She left the stove and took the short woman in her arms, held her for a long moment. "Let me see, how far along are you now?"

"A little over four months now."

"Too early for me to tell girl or boy. You ain't gonna get very big, being your first one. I should be able to tell by the fifth month. Maybe by the time school out for the summer."

"Where is everybody?" Rosanna asked.

"Yo daddy got the boys down at the pond, drownin' worms. Ain't no fish in the pond with them alligators."

"How many alligators he got?" Jamaria asked, peeking out the window at the pond.

"Ain't but a half dozen or so now," Rosie Franklin answered. "Ben kills any more of them off before breedin' season ever' year. He always kill off the biggest ones, don't let 'em get too big. They get too dangerous when they get real big."

"Do they ever get past the fence?"

"No, never have. Ben would shoot it if one ever did, though. Come on, les' feed these younguns so when the menfolk get back we can eat in peace. The kids can go upstairs and play while we eat."

Women rounded up the children, washed faces and hands, made plates with each child deciding what they wanted and put them at low tables on the screened-in porch. The women sat in chairs around the walls of the porch, glasses of iced tea at hand, and talked while the children ate.

"Jamaria, that's a pretty little girl you got." Rosie Franklin waved toward Kacy. "She resembles you anough to be yourn."

"That's what I told her, Mama," Rosanna said. "I think it's why he left her with Jamaria."

"Shh," Jamaria shushed them. "She gon hear you."

"We talk later."

The children finished eating. They took their plates into the kitchen, scraped them into the compost bucket, put the plates and glasses into the sink, and washed their hands. Bigger kids helped the smaller ones.

"How do you get them to do that?" Jamaria asked in awe of the children's efficiency cleaning up their table.

"Mama beats them three times a day," Rosanna said, without missing a beat between question and answer.

All five of the daughters-in-law burst into laughter.

"That's what Mama Rosie told me when I asked," Susie, the youngest of her daughters-in-law, said. "I ain't never seen her lay a hand on any one of them."
"I used to wish she would just go 'head and beat me," Rosanna said. "She made me practice washing dishes, and washing faces, and saying yes ma'am, and everything so many times, a beating would've been a blessing."

"You wouldn't'a learned anythin' from a beatin', 'cept hatred, maybe," Mama Rosie said. "Repeatin' and doin' over and over, you learned the right way, and patience, and a whole lot of other things'."

"True, Mama, true. Sure was tough at the time."

"At the time ain't the important part. You only a youngun for a little while. You grown for a long time, and you don't forget the lessons you learned as a youngun."

"You right, Mama Rosie," the women all conceded, nodding and saying together.

The children finished clearing their table as the men came stomping into the porch.

"When's supper, Mama? We thought Daddy never would turn us loose to come eat," the men came complaining.

"Whoa." Mama Rosie stopped the men. "Did you catch anything?"

"We kept enough for you and Daddy a mess. He wouldn't let us keep any more," Frank, the oldest boy, said.

"Yeah, he said if we couldn't catch enough for all, then you and him was the only ones to

eat fish," John said. The other boys laughed.

"He said to leave enough for the alligators, else they'd start climbing the fence." Beau lead the laughter.

"Well, get out there and clean them fish and wash y'all's face and hands 'fore y'all come in here to eat at my table." Mama Rosie herded them back out the door. The boys knew better than to argue.

The women took time to gather the children and take them upstairs to the playroom. Older children, in charge of play, turned on the television in one room for the ones who wanted to watch. Mothers threatened the existence of the ones who didn't behave.

Men and women came together in the large dining room, sat beside each other, Rosanna and Jamaria across the table from each other, on the left and right of Mr. Franklin. Everyone around the table joined hands and he said grace. At the end, everyone around the table squeezed the hands they were holding.

Mr. Franklin's glance swept the faces around the table, to Mama Rosie. "Well, Mama, ain't it wonderful to have our whole family home once more? All five of the boys and their families and now we got both the girls: the one we birthed and the one we took into our hearts. Jes don't get no better than this."

Jamaria, tears stinging, brought her napkin to her eyes. "Thank you, Papa Ben. I'm sorry I ain't been to see y'all in such a long time. I don't have any excuse, I'm jes sorry."

"Baby girl, don't say sorry to us." He put his hand

over hers. "Jes, don't be this long again."

"I tried to tell her, Daddy," Rosanna said. "She wouldn't listen to me."

"I know you did, baby," Papa said. "Sometimes we jes need to get our folks home to have a talk, y'know?" Everyone around the table nodded, began passing food around the table, and eating.

Jamaria's tears flowed for a moment; she wiped her eyes with the napkin and began filling her plate as the bowls passed the table. Table talk centered around the children, jobs, and school letting out for the summer in less than a month.

The last day of school, Kacy was excited. "You gonna pick me up? Promise? By lunchtime, promise?" she kept repeating as they creeped along in line for her to get out of the car at school.

Jamaria stopped the car, leaned over and took the girl's face between her hands. "I promise I be here. We'll go out to Mama Rosie's for lunch, then I go back to work."
Kacy's sigh of relief audible as she hugged Jamaria and turned to get out of the car.

At Mama Rosie's later, cars arrived from all elementary in the county.

"Come on in and git ready to eat." Mama Rosie hugged each child as they came through the screened porch.

"You don' know how much I 'preciate you doing

this," Jamaria whispered, as she and Kacy came through the door.

"Don' you worry. These other folk pay me gracious plenty and they happy to," Mama Rosie whispered to Jamarie and smiled.

"Come on in, everybody." Mama Rosie raised her voice so everyone heard. "Some of you going back to work. Come on in and get to eating, soon as we say grace."

Each mother sat beside or between her children. After grace, dishes passed around, and everyone began to eat while keeping up happy chatter. The children ranged in age from thirteen to infants. Children over thirteen worked on farms or for family members in their businesses, at least part of the summer. The oldest children at Mama Rosie's, helped care for the younger ones, at least a dozen any given day: all family, or like Kacy, nearly family.

Kacy followed Jamaria to her car. "You gonna be okay?" the woman asked.

"Yeah, this gon be fun."

"You mind Mama Rosie, now."

Yesum, I will. You coming to get me after work, ain't you?"

"Yes, baby girl, I will be here directly after work. I won't never let you stay nowhere but with me, if I can help."

Kacy smiled, hugged her, turned, and ran back to the house.

***

The letter came addressed to Jamaria three days before school started toward the end of August, the heat oppressive in the tiny south Georgia town. She and Kacy sat on the porch, talking about school supplies and whether Kacy needed a book bag for first grade.

"Guess I need to waddle out an' get my mail," Jamaria said.

"I get it for you," Kacy offered, jumped off the low porch and ran. Running back with the handful of ads, assorted flyers and bills, she handed them to Jamaria. The woman leafed through them and laid them on the floor, stopped, glanced back through the handful of mail and went back through them more slowly. One envelope caught her attention. She lay the largest group on the floor, stood to go into the house, leaned over, picked up the other mail, and started into the house.

"Where you goin'?" Kacy asked.

"Jes goin' to open some of these bills."

"You comin' back?"

"Yeah, I be back. Stay out here where it a mite cooler."

Inside, Jamaria made two glasses of iced tea and drank deeply from one. She slid a paring knife under the flap of the suspicious envelope. From Huntsville Prison, Huntsville, Alabama, Montre Desmonte, but she would have known without his name; who else?

"My dear Jammarie, I know you ain't gon believ dis, but I don found mysef in prison. Dey say I frawded some woman outn her money. Now you no me beter dan dat. I didn' do it. But dey foun me guilty. I gone be here a long time, mayb 10 years. Ples keep car of my babes Kacy and the babe what you got in you. I don no 'bout them other babes, but I no yourn is mine.
Lov, Montre Desmonte"

Jamaria sat heavily in a kitchen chair and let her tears flow. How can I tell that child? What will I tell her? Can I take care of these babies by myself? She allowed herself a few moments of self-pity and wiped her face with a cool, damp paper towel. Putting the envelope under dishtowels in a bottom drawer, she refilled her glass with iced tea, picked up both glasses, and went back to the porch, handing one to Kacy.

"Sweetie," she said, after a moment, "why don' you start calling me Mama when you go back to school? Wouldn't it be easier than having to 'splain to all yo friends at school who we are to each other?"

"You mean I can do that 'thout you really being my Mama? What you reckon my Daddy say?"

"Well, seems like a long time 'fore he gets back, but

we can ask him when he does. What

you say?"

"I think I like that," Kacy said, after a long pause. "Some of them nasty boys in kindygarden use to make fun of me not havin' a mama or a daddy. Some of them didn' have no daddy neither. Now when I get in first grade, I can have a mama, too."

Watching the sunset, Kacy remarked, "Look at them pretty colors, all pink and purple and yellow and orange. Ain't they pretty, Mama? I think I'm gonna color that when I get home tomorrow."

"That's a good idea, baby girl." Jamaria gazed at the girl with love. The colors almost finished, she picked up her glass and said, "Let's go in the house. These skeeters gonna tote us off." She reached for Kacy's glass, but the girl picked it up and opened the front door.

After Kacy's bath, lying in bed, she asked, "Did we say I gonna git a book bag or not?"

Jamaria laughed. "I don't think we said. If you think you need one, les git you one."

"Good night, Mama." The girl lowered her head, not looking at Jamaria.

"Good night, Kacy. I love you, girl." She leaned over and kissed the child's cheek.

"Like Jesus?"

"Like a mama." Jamaria kissed Kacy's cheek again, raised herself off the side of the bed, and waddled out of the room, closing the door behind her.

The phone rang as soon as Jamaria sat in her chair in the living room. Rosanna, excited about something.

"Slow down, I can't understand nothing you saying."

"You shoulda been at church tonight," Rosanna said, still fast, but Jamaria finally understood.

"Why, what's going on?"

"They was this fine looking man. You shoulda seen him."

"Why don't you take him? Who is he?"

"That's what I'm trying to tell you. He the preacher's brother. He moved down here 'cause his wife died two years ago. Her mother was staying with him to help with his younguns. She got sick and went in the nursing home, up in Detroit, or one of them foreign places."

"What does he do?"

"He a preacher, too. Reverend Grimes gonna recommend him for a church down in Fargo. They have been needing a preacher for a the long time."

"Who gonna take care of the chiluns now?"

88

"Oh, they all old enough to be in school, and he can be home with them after school."

"So what does this man look like?"

"Well, you wouldn' never take them for brothers." Rosanna laughed her boisterous, full blown laugh.

"Where he staying?"

"Now they staying with the Reverend and his wife. The church in Fargo has a house for their preacher, so he may be moving 'fore long." A pause while Rosanna took a deep breath. "I ain't tole you the best part."

"What? Tell me."

"James ask me if the Reverend and his wife keep his kids, would I go out to eat with him." She started screaming and Jamaria screamed with her, stopped, afraid she awaken Kacy.

"Oh, oh, oh, my bes' friend got herself a boyfriend. I'm so happy for you!"

"No, ain't nothing like that, yet. He been here a month now .All those other womens been looking at him like they want to eat him with a spoon, and I the one he ask. Do you think he's looking for a mama for his chiluns?"

"I think if that's what he wanted, he'd'a done it a long time ago. Be happy for youself."

"Ya think so?"

"Yeah, I do. If he ask you out, then you is the one he want to go out with."

"Well, if I go out with him, I'm'a ask him. I will."

"You sure will, I know you." They both laughed.

Two weeks later, Jamaria left work in labor. She picked Kacy up at school and drove her to Mama Rosie's house, called Rosanna at work, and drove herself to the hospital against the advice of Mama Rosie and Papa Ben.

Walking into the emergency entrance of the hospital, her water broke.

"Who brought you here?" The nurse looked behind Jamaria, down the hall for someone to help.

I brought myself," Jamaria answered, doubling over in pain for the first time.

"How did you?"

"That's the first bad pain I had," she gasped.

"Let's put you in a wheelchair and get you admitted. We'll need to get you in a room soon, too."
As the pains came harder and longer, Jamaria doubled over in agony. When she saw Rosanna coming down the hall in her uniform, she almost smiled.

"I knew you'd be here, I did." Jamaria welcomed Rosanna's hug as she arrived at the wheelchair.

Rosanna glared at the admitting clerk. "Can't you let them take her to a room? I'll finish this for you." She motioned for the nurse to take Jamaria away and took the insurance papers from her hand.

The nurse wheeled Jamaria away and down the hall toward the maternity rooms. By the time Rosanna got to her, Jamaria, settling in bed, had been checked by the nurses. The big woman took her hand. "Are you okay?"

"Yeah, they told me won't gone be long. Would'a scared me to death, if I'd'a knowed how far along I was when I got here." They laughed until Jamaria doubled over with pain. She grabbed Rosanna's hand and squeezed.

The pain easing, Jamaria laid back on the bed. Rosanna got a cloth, wet with cool water.

As she brought the cloth to Jamaria, a tall, slim black man knocked and pushed the door open. "Rosanna, here you are. Your mother said I would find you here."

Rosanna turned to him. "Come on in, let me introduce you to my best friend in the world.

This here is Jamaria Williston. She the one I been telling you about."

"I'm pleased to meet you, Miss Jamaria Williston. Any friend of Rosanna is a friend of mine. I'm James Grimes, but my friends call me Jimmy. I'm your Reverend Grimes' younger brother, but please call me Jimmy."

"I'm pleased to meet you, Brother Jimmy. Rosanna been my best friend for many years, since before my mama died when I was about twelve. I lived with Mama Rosie and Papa Ben 'til I graduated. I love their family like they mine." She tried to smile, but grabbed Rosanna's hand and squeezed again as another pain hit her.

He took her other hand. "My wife birthed three babies holding onto my hand, why don't you let me help you a little?"

Rosanna went to refresh the cloth with cool water, his eyes followed her. "Ain't Rosanna something? She's a beautiful woman.."

Jamaria examined him to be sure he was sincere. His eyes told her he meant his words. Her sigh of relief not about her pain.

A nurse stuck her head in the door. "Let me check, may be time to move her to the delivery room. I need you two to leave the room for a few minutes." Rosanna and James left the room, hesitating.

The nurse came running out the door, calling to the other nurses, "Isn't the doctor still here? Get him down here, NOW."

Rosanna and James went to Jamaria and took her hands.

"What did she say?" Rosanna asked.

"I think she say the baby is coming," Jamaria's voice barely above a whisper and quaking.

CHAPTER 3

The nurses came running, prepared the bed to move to the delivery room. James and Rosanna followed and stood outside the door, waiting for news.

Within fifteen minutes, the doctor ran into the delivery room, another nurse ran in and a different nurse came out holding the baby.

"A boy." She held him toward the couple briefly and scurried away to the nursery. James put his arm around Rosanna and smiled at her.

"Jamaria will be happy." He pulled the big woman closer.

"Why you think?"

"Didn't she say she would like for Kacy to have a little brother?"

"I think she did. I forgot. Wonder how long 'fore we can see her?"

"Won't be long. We can go wait in her room. They'll bring her back as soon as they finish in the delivery room."

James and Rosanna went to get Kacy after they spent a little time with Jamaria back in her room. When they brought Kacy into the room, Jamaria grinning, holding the baby, and exclaiming about how beautiful he was.

"What you gonna name him?" Kacy asked. "You gonna name him Montre after our daddy?"

"No, if it been a girl, I'd name her Montay. But I'm gonna name him Monty."

"Are you going to give him a middle name?" James asked.

"Williston, my name can be his middle name"

"Mon-ty Wil-lis-ton Day-mon-tay." Rosanna pronounced each syllable separately. "A mouthful."

"This little guy is going to live up to his name." James chuckled.

"This baby is almos' pretty as his big sister," Rosanna said, picking Kacy up and putting her on the bed beside Jamaria. Kacy beamed, leaned over and gazed at Monty.

"My face ain't wrinkle' up."

"Give him a few days, and his won't be either."

"Kin I hold him when we git him home?"

"Oh, yeah. I 'spect you gone be holding him a good bit 'fore he gets big enough to git 'round on his own," Rosanna said. "We need to git you back to Mama's house so you can git supper and git ready for bed. Papa'll bring you back tomorrow, right after school."

"You ain't gon bring me?"

"I'll be working, but Papa'll bring you, and take you back. Jamaria'll be going home in a day or so, and you can go home, too."

"Okay." Kacy leaned over the baby and hugged Jamaria. "I love you, Mama. We be back tomorrow."

"I love you, too, baby girl." Jamaria's eyes shone with unshed tears of joy as she smiled at Kacy.

James and Rosanna came to take Jamaria home from the hospital, Rosanna to drive Jamaria' car.

"Girl, this seat is set for a midget," Rosanna told her, when she tried to get into the car. "I'm'a move it befo' I can even git in." They laughed as Rosanna fiddled with the seat and the steering wheel until she could drive Jamaria's car. "My chin is on my knees, but the best I can do. How in the world did you drive yo'self to the hospital?"

"Well, I'm not six feet tall. Lucky fo you, James is a head taller than you."

"Ain't it?" Rosanna burst into laughter. "I met his children last week. We waited, I wanted to be sure we liked each other enough. Well, I've seen them at church, but not met them officially. He introduce me, and we went out to eat. The boy, he the oldest, he say . . . he say to me, 'You almost as tall as my mama'. I been thinking I'm too tall, and too big, and . . . ."

"Rosanna," Jamaria said, putting her hand on her friend's shoulder. "Don't do this to yo'sef. Jimmy like you for you. Don' put yo'sef down."

"Maybe he do, jes maybe he do." She smiled. "That boy of his, he taller than you, but ain't saying much. Half the world taller than you, and the other half is babies." Her laughter filled the car with mirth, startled the baby, and caused Jamaria to join.

As Jamaria walked into her house it was transformed, television set now in the living

room. In her bedroom, a crib, and to the side a small chest of drawers filled with baby clothes, and other needed accessories. Several packages of disposable diapers sat on top.

"Who did all this?"

"Your family." Rosanna beamed.

"Your family?"

"Our family."

Jamaria burst into tears, still holding Monty. Jimmy took the baby from her.

"Here, let me hold the little fellow while the two of you have a crying moment." He carried the baby to the couch and sat. He began singing to him, crooning.
Jamaria reached up to hug Rosanna; they held the hug for a long time, both in tears. Releasing each other, they sat on either side of Jimmy, looking at the baby.
"Les go sit on the porch," Jamaria suggested. "A

mite cooler outside, I think."

Jimmy started to hand Monty to her, but she motioned for him to keep him. Jimmy gave Rosanna a quizzical glance, but held the baby as they walked to the porch, taking seats in the rocking chairs.

"A little breeze out here, feels good," Jimmy commented, rocking.

Rosanna followed Jimmy. "Ya know, they's an old superstition a baby be like the first person carries it out of the house. Jamaria want the baby to be like you."

"Is that right? Well, I consider it a real compliment. Thank you, Jamaria." He ducked his head, embarrassed.

"I can't say as I want him to be like his daddy, and I think you a fine man. I hope my friend here know, too."

Rosanna stood. "Let me go make us some iced tea. Guess I need to make a fresh batch?
Jamaria smiled up at her friend. "Yes, pour the stuff in the refrigerator out and start over."

With Rosanna gone into the house, Jamaria said, "Guess I'll go check the mailbox. Probly stuffed full."

"I'll go for you, if you want," Jimmy offered.

"I need to move around. Layin' in bed at the hospital

made me sore, kinda stove up."

She stepped gingerly off the porch and toddled out to the mailbox, taking everything out.
"Whew, even a little walkin' tired me out."

"It'll get better every day."

Leafing through the mail, Jamaria paid little attention to Jimmy's comment. She pulled out the envelope from Huntsville Prison and frowned.

"Something you didn't expect?" Jimmy asked.

"From the baby daddy."

"Oh?"

"He in prison. I never told nobody."

"Did you hold this inside all this time?"

"I only found out a few weeks ago. I didn't know how to tell Kacy her daddy gone be in prison ten years."
"And you're carrying all this in your heart by yourself. Did you even talk to Rosanna?" Jimmy asked.
"No, she been so happy, I didn't want to bring her down and be a burden with my problems."

"She'll be upset with you for not talking to her. Let's go in and discuss the situation. We can pray about this. Our Lord may have something to help us." Jimmy stood with the baby, and Jamaria carried mail in her arm.

Rosanna looked at them with trepidation in her eyes as they walked into the kitchen.

"Let me take Monty." Jamaria reached for the baby. "I'll put him to bed, and we can talk."

"What this about?" Rosanna asked Jimmy.

"Jamaria will tell you when she gets back. Is the iced tea ready? Anything I can do to help?"

He opened a cabinet, pulled out a plate of cookies Mama Rosie had made and covered
with plastic wrap.

"I turned the fan on," Jamaria said, coming back in the kitchen. "Did I have those cookies?"

"No," Rosanna said, and laughed. "Mama made these, but your family brought some groceries, too. You don't need to go the grocery store any time soon."

Jamaria got glasses from the cabinet, filled them with ice, and poured tea. They sat at the table without speaking. She took the first letter received from Montre and motioned for the two of them to read. She took the new letter and slit the opening with a paring knife.

"My deer Jammaria:
I no I can't rightly ask this of yu. But wood yu bring my babes to see me. I wont ask this of yu mor'n onct. That woman I frawded? Her cusin here too. He want to kill me. I jus want to see my babes and

yu 1 mor tim.
Lov Montre Desmonte"

After reading silently, and Rosanna and James read the first letter, Jamaria handed the new letter to them.

"Whatchu gonna do?" Rosanna asked, after reading.

"I ain't even told Kacy he's in prison. How can I tell her he want us to go over there?" She drank from her glass and absently took a cookie from the plate.

"Why don't you let me do it for you?" Jimmy asked. "As the children's director in our church in Detroit, I had experience telling children bad news. You and Rosanna can answer questions."

"James, what a wonderful idea," Rosanna said.

"How can I thank you?" Jamaria burst into tears, reached for a paper towel from the counter, and went to the front porch.

Rosanna and Jimmy refilled their glasses and followed her.

They listened for the baby, talked about the church, when Jamaria would go back to work, Kacy, and other things, until Papa Ben drove up with Kacy in his pickup truck.

"We didn't know if you would get home befo' the bus run," Papa Ben said. After the greetings, after Kacy ran in to check on the baby and get a snack, he left to do chores.

Sitting around the table, glasses of fresh iced tea all round, Jimmy asked, "Jamaria, do
you want me to talk with everyone here?" She nodded, glancing at Kacy. Jimmy continued, "May I hold the letters, please."Jamaria got both letters and returned to sit.

"Kacy." Jimmy got her full attention. "Your Mama Jamaria got two letters from your Daddy. She wants me to read them and talk to you about them. Would you like me to read them to you?"

"Yes, sir." Kacy's voice trembled.

James Grimes read the letters as though letter perfect, grammar perfect and heartfelt. When he finished, Kacy studied him for a long moment.

"My daddy didn't write them letters," she said, softly. "He ain't in no prison."

Jamaria started to protest, but Jimmy held his hand to quiet her. "Yes, he did, Kacy. The return address, here, on the envelopes, says Huntsville Prison. His name is on both of them."

"Where that place is?"

"In Alabama."

"Where we?"

"We're in Georgia, south east Georgia, a long way from Alabama."

Kacy turned and looked at Jamaria. "Can we go?"

"Not right away," Jimmy answered for Jamaria. "Your mama just got out of the hospital today. She needs to rest a while, and the baby doesn't need to travel. In a couple of weeks or a month."

"Can we, Mama, can we?"

"You heard Mr. Jimmy, in a couple of weeks or a month." Jamaria put her arm around the girl, hugging her close. She looked at Rosanna and smiled. Not as hard as I thought.

***

Two weeks later, Jimmy and Rosanna drove Jamaria, Kacy and Monty to Huntsville to visit Montre. They left before dawn and drove all morning, arriving after noon.

Jamaria was embarrassed for herself and Kacy at the search endured to visit Montre. We won't be making this visit again, she thought.

"Daddy!" Kacy screamed when seeing him, but stopped short as she got a good look.

The bloating appeared to Jamaria of eating too much and evidence of old bruises, too. Montre took Kacy in his arms and picked her up. He motioned for Jamaria to sit at a picnic table and tried to hug her. Jamaria pulled away and uncovered Monty for him to view.

"Did you drive over here by yo'sef?" Montre asked.

"No, Rosanna and her boyfriend brought us."

"Rosanna got a boyfrien'? Wid her big, ol', ugly sef?"

"Miss Rosanna ain't ugly." Kacy defended her friend. "Mr. Jimmy is nice."

Jamaria gazed directly at Montre. "Don't make me sorry I come here."

"No, no, I'm sorry I said anythin'," he protested. "I'm jes surprised, dat's all."

"We can't stay long." Jamaria said, looking at the baby. "I jes wanted you to see the baby once. We won't be making a drive again any time soon."

A toddler across the room started screaming so loud, everyone quieted, searching for the reason for the child's screams. Its mother sat, kissing the man she visited, ignoring the child. Another woman, close by, raced over to the couple, slapped the two of them, screamed curses at them, and returned to her seat. Prison guards raced to the women as the mother of the toddler reached the woman who slapped her, grabbed the woman's hair, and snatching her backward. The two women fell to the floor, and the guards tried to separate them.

Most of the visitors in the room began surrounding the two women, screaming encouragement for one or the other. Guards couldn't get to the women to separate them.

Announcements began over the public address system, but ignored. Guards pushed through, pulled the women apart, dragged them to different areas. More guards came, ushering visitors out the exit doors. They came to get Jamaria and Kacy and led them out, too.

"All visitors must leave." The guards repeated over and over, refused to answer questions or acknowledge anyone.

"Write me a letter," Montre called as Jamaria and the children were pushed to the door.

Kacy cried as they left. Jamaria tried to comfort her as she carried Monty. Handing Monty to Rosanna, she knelt and took Kacy in her arms.

"You weren't there long," Jimmy commented.

"There was a problem," Jamaria said.

"Let's go," Rosanna suggested. "We can talk about all this later." She stared at the other visitors, mostly women, who exited the prison. Some still arguing, still trying to fight.

A couple of weeks before Christmas, Monty cooed and tried to sit when propped up in a corner of the couch. Kacy helped Jamaria set up the tree with sparkling multi-color lights, buy and wrap inexpensive gifts for everyone. They made ornaments; Monty laughed aloud at them.

"Can I sen' my Daddy some of these?" Kacy asked.

"Yeah, sure, baby, you can. We'll make some to send him. We'll ask Mr. Jimmy to take a picture of you and Monty to send him, too."

Pictures taken, developed, ornaments readied, and the package sent within a couple of days.

On Christmas morning, after Santa Claus came during the night to Jamaria's house and left gifts for Kacy and Monty, they opened packages. The girl opened the baby's gifts and showed him all the things in his packages. This is what Christmas is about, Jamaria mused, I never dreamed what I missed.

With the packages opened and the wrapping paper thrown away, they went to spend the day with Rosanna's family. Walking in the door, Kacy stared. "Wow, what a big Christmas tree, and pretty, too."

Soon after Jamaria arrived, Jimmy came with his three children, the Franklin's five boys already arrived with their combined sixteen children. Mama Rosie sent all the children upstairs to play, leaving the adults to talk before lunch, gift opening after lunch.

Riding home, Kacy falling asleep in the car, Monty slept. "Mama," Kacy mumbled. "I ain't never had a Christmas like this. Is it always like this 'round here?"

"Well, none of the kids at Christmas were mine before, but it always special at Mama Rosie's and Papa Ben's."

"I want to stay wid you forever." Kacy's head drifted over as they drove into their short driveway.

"Come on, sweet girl. We got to get you and this baby in the house 'before y'all get to sleep." Jamaria carried Monty, and got Kacy in the house with a hand on her shoulder.

Jamaria sat, after putting the children to bed, with a glass of tea. Even with Mama Rosie keeping the kids for me, how am I ever going to make ends meet? Never thought it would be this hard. Less than a thousand dollars put away and living from payday to payday. What if one of them gets sick? Rosanna came for supper the next evening; Jimmy visiting the church in Fargo. The entire congregation interested in meeting him, several members ready to invite him to move to their tiny town.

"What am I going to do, Rosanna?" Jamaria started after the children slept. They discussed her finances before, seemed to be no solution.

Rosanna laughed. "Well, quit yo' job and get welfare. Those folk seem to get along all right."

Jamaria glanced at her from the corner of her eye. "That ain't even funny. I ain't fixing to do something stupid."

"I'm jes teasing. You gonna do jes fine. The Lord gone provide for you, jes like he been doing. He ain't gon put something on you you can't handle."

"In my heart I know, but every time my head keep

108

saying, you can't spend all this paycheck, something comes up."

"I know, honey. The Lord's gonna take care of you. I better be going, work at seven in the morning. You get these babies to Mama so you can be at work by eight, don't you?"

"Yeah, what would I do without my big sister? You make me sure I can go on. Thanks, Rosanna." She hugged her friend as they parted at the door, waited until she cranked her car, closed and locked the door.

The fifth day into the new year, cold and rainy, Kacy climbed on the school bus and Jamaria left with Monty, taking him to Mama Rosie. The baby burst into smiles when he spotted her face, which made Jamaria happy and sad. Happy because Mama Rosie took good care of him, sad knowing she couldn't be with him all day.

"I'm sorry to be in such a hurry, Mama Rosie." She handed Monty to the older woman. "My boss been givin' me a hard time about bein' late."

"Maybe he can a'just your time a little bit."

"He don't seem to be willing." Jamaria hurried out.

When Jamaria picked Monty up, she hugged Mama Rosie. The older woman walked out to the car with them and placed a casserole dish on the back seat. "Jes a little somethin' to help with yo' supper." She hugged Kacy.

At home, Jamaria warmed the casserole while she got Monty fed and ready for bed. Kacy read to her while teasing Monty with the words in her book. They laughed at his giggle, enjoying the family life fallen into over the months.

After eating, Kacy helped put Monty to bed, wash dishes, and started to bed.

"Can I watch TV?" Kacy asked.

"No, baby, bedtime."

"All my friends do."
"They must stay up late, or they watch in the afternoon. In this house, I don't even stay up late. As soon as you go to sleep, I go to bed, too."

"I bet they don' have as much fun as we do. Good night, Mama." They laughed together.

"Good night, my sweet girl." They hugged goodnight.

Jamaria grabbed an unbrella and a flashlight, went out the front door and hurried through the drizzling rain to the mailbox. Back on the porch, she shook the umbrella, took it into the house, knowing she would need it the next day. She lay the flashlight and mail on the table, put the umbrella in the mop bucket, picked up the mail, flipping through quickly. After Christmas sales, and I got no money. Always the way?

Her hand on the large, thick envelope told her the difference before her eyes checked the address, the return address. Huntsville, Alabama. Huntsville Prison. Not Montre Desmonte. William T. Brink, Warden. Oh, my God.

CHAPTER 4

Jamaria turned the envelope over and over in her hands. She pressed on the corners, the middle, shook it. Didn't make sense she would get a package like this from the warden, not Montre. Afraid to look at the contents, at last she took a paring knife and slit the seal. She pulled everything from the envelope, looking to be sure. There was the picture she had sent at Christmas, the ornaments she and Kacy made and sent to Montre, another, smaller envelope sealed. A different envelope, typed, not handwritten, with the address of the prison, also with the warden's name.

She opened the typed one with the warden's name. This one might be the one with the worst news. She spied the signature first, signed by the warden. Two pages, she started to read. She read once, nothing registered in her mind. She picked up her phone.

"Rosanna, I got a letter. It's late, but can you come over here?"

"Why you sound so funny?"

"I need you to come read this letter for me."

"I'll call Jimmy, too."

"Okay." Jamaria hung up the phone, sat staring a long while until a tentative knock on the door.

"Jamaria," Jimmy called, as another set of headlights turned into her driveway.

Rosanna jumped from her car and came running across the porch to the door. "Baby, are you okay?"

Jimmy and Rosanna came through the door and took her in their arms together.

Jimmy glanced at Rosanna. "Let's come sit down, and we can figure out what's going on." He led them into the living room.

"Where the letter you talking 'bout?" Rosanna asked.

"On the table." Jamaria started to get up.

"I'll get it." Jimmy brought everything from the envelope into the living room and spread things on the coffee table. He held the warden's letter, reading through twice, and handed the letter to Rosanna.

No one said anything until she finished reading the letter.

"This other envelope contains all his personal effects, but there's not much." Jimmy handed it to Jamaria. "He included a copy of Montre's death certificate with his letter. Says he died from cardiac arrest, but the beating from the woman's cousin and his friends must have caused his heart to stop. I'm so sorry Jamaria. This is going to be difficult for Kacy. Monty won't ever know his daddy, but this will be difficult for Kacy."
"He spent two days in their hospital, must have

suffered a lot." Jamaria buried her head in her hands.

"No." Rosanna pointed out. "He was in a coma. He didn' feel nothin', I don' think. Your address is the only one they found in his cell. Do you know if there's any more family?"

Jamaria shook her head. "He ain't never talk about no more family 'cept Kacy and her mama. Never talk much 'bout his mama an' daddy, just in passing."

"They already buried him at the prison, but if you want to move his body somewhere close to here, we can probably arrange that," Jimmy said, reaching out, putting his hand over Jamaria's.

"I don't have any money for such as that. Any money I get goes to take care of these babies," Jamaria said.

"The church might be able to help you," Rosanna said.

"I can't ask them. Might come a time I need them for something, and I shore don't want to use up any help I might can git from them."

"Now, that ain't the way the church work," Rosanna said.

"That the way I am. I can't thank y'all enough for coming tonight. I jes couldn't know what to do. I needed my friends." Tears fell freely by the time she finished, and Jamaria stood to get a towel from the kitchen.

Jimmy and Rosanna followed her into the kitchen. "Finding out a parent of your children died is difficult at any time. Even in your case where you weren't living with him, he's still their father. But things get easier, day by day. Wait until Rosanna and I can be with you to tell Kacy. Might make the telling a little easier."

"Okay, y'all come for supper tomorrow night." Still wiping her tears, but the flow stopped.

Jimmy glanced at Rosanna, she nodded, he said, "We'll be here."

Mildred Peterson, principal at Kacy's school sent a note home with the girl the day she

found her crying in the girls' restroom. She asked Jamaria to come visit on her next day off work.

Jamaria carried Monty on her hip, followed Kacy into the school. "You can go on to yo' classroom, Kacy. I need to talk with Miss Mildred. I'll pick you up this afternoon. Love ya."

She leaned down for Kacy to hug her and the baby. Monty giggled as Kacy ran off toward her classroom.

"Certainly looks like a happy baby." Mildred she came around the counter and led Jamaria toward her office.

"He is," Jamaria said, a little hesitant, wondering

what this meeting could be about.

"Oh, Jamaria, I hope you aren't concerned about this meeting. It's nothing to worry about." Mildred motioned for her to sit. "I wanted to talk to you about how Kacy is getting along since she got the news about her daddy." She hesitated. "And about some other things.

"Kacy havin' a hard time. But you probally know. I don' have the money to move his body to a cemetery here and she wantin' to go to his grave. I tole her we go when school out."

"She told me. If you need some financial assistance, I can suggest a couple of things. Welfare, of course, but less than you make working."

Jamaria waved her hand. "I'm not interested, no ma'am."

"I knew you wouldn't be. But there are other things. Have you applied for Social Security for the children?"

"That for old people."

"It's also for children whose parents are disabled or deceased. With the letters from Montre, you should be able to get it for the children."

"Is that so?"

"Yes, take the letters to the Social Security office and apply for survivors benefits. They'll tell you what else you might need. I don't have any idea how much money you would get, but . . ."

"Anything I can git for the children would help me take care of them better." Tears came

to Jamaria, but she refused to shed them. "Thank you so much, Miss Mildred. I don' know how to tell you how much I 'preciate you tellin' me this. I'm going straight home and getting' the papers and go now."

"Let me give you a copy of his registration form for Kacy. He used his last name for her. Should count for something."

The big-bellied man at the Social Security office scanned at all the papers Jamaria brought, made copies of them, filled out a multitude of forms, she signed them, and he told her she would receive a decision from them soon. He refused to answer questions, telling her he only took applications, not processed them. She left not knowing any more than she did when she arrived.

The wait seemed interminable, but Jamaria figured barring any major catastrophes she would be able to continue as she had been, with the help from God and her friends.

On Valentine's Day, Kacy brought her a card she made in school, and one for Monty, too. Jamaria bought cupcakes from the store where she worked. They had a family party before the children went to bed. Shortly after the children fell asleep, and she about to go to bed, there came a knock on her door.

Before she opened the door, Rosanna barged in, dragging Jimmy behind her. "Jamaria, you ain't never gon believe this. Let me tell you!"

"Now, sweetheart, why wouldn't she believe this?" Jimmy put his arm around Rosanna.

"What?" Jamaria asked, leading them into the living room, motioning for them to sit. "Tell me."

Rosanna stretched her left arm out and showed Jamaria her ring finger, an engagement ring with a small diamond.

"We getting' married!" She squealed, shaking her hand in her friend's face.

Jamaria jumped up and hugged her friend and Jimmy. "I'm so happy for y'all. When this gonna happen?"

"Soon." Jimmy finally got a word in. "I'm moving to Fargo next week and they want us to be married in the church the week after."

"Can you get ready?" Jamaria asked.
"If you he'p me, I can. I need you to go with me, get a dress, and everything I need."

"What you gon do 'bout yo' job?"

"That the best part. I'm quitting the nursing home. I'm gonna be the school nurse in Fargo, only six hours a day."

"I'm gone miss you." Jamaria's tears forming.

Jimmy laughed. "You talk like it's a long way, only about twenty miles from here. The two of you can visit anytime you want." He put his arm around Rosanna.

"You right," Rosanna said, and they all laughed.

***

The day of the wedding dawned bright, clear with a forecast of high seventies. Late February in south Georgia, sometimes a precursor to an early spring, sometimes a false alarm.

Guests for the wedding were on the road to Fargo early. Everyone wanted to be early, in time for the wedding party pictures being taken. The ceremony scheduled for eleven, and the church would be serving lunch in the fellowship hall.

Rosanna was dressed in a tea length, pale mauve dress with long sleeves, and a square neckline. She squeezed her mother's hand until Jamaria arrived.
"Oh, I'm so glad you here," Mama Rosie said, removing her hand from Rosanna's, stretching, rubbing her hands together. "I need to find all those grands of mine. You gon be here with Rosanna? Who got yo babies?"

"Miss Mildred got Kacy, and Susie took Monty." Jamaria motioned for Rosanna to sit to work on the placement of her hat.

"My Susie?" Mama Rosie threw her hands in the air. "My Beau's wife?"

Jamaria nodded with a bobby pin in her mouth.

"Lawd let me go get that baby 'fore she leave him in a flower pot. Girl so absent minded."

Rosanna and Jamaria laughed as Mama Rosie scuttled out of the room.

Jamaria hugged Rosanna from behind. "Rosanna, I'm so happy for you today. I could jes bust."

She continued working on the hat until she realized her friend had not responded.

Going around, she found Rosanna holding her tears in.

"Oh, honey, you go 'head and cry if you need to. This s'posed to be a happy day. They be happy tears." She grabbed tissues from the dresser in the bride's room and handed them to her friend. She took some for herself.

"Jamaria, this ought to be you, getting married, bein' happy . . . . " Rosanna dabbed at the tears rolling down her cheeks.

"No, no, Rosanna. You deserve all the happiness in the world. You always been the one who stand by your family, your friends, the people you work with." Jamaria took her friend's hand. "You the best friend anybody ever ask for, but you even better as a sister. I'm proud to be your, what you call 'matron of honor?' Well that's me, cause I honor you as my friend, and my sister, every day. I couldn't have made it through this last year without you." Using the tissues in her hand, she wiped tears.

Both shedding tears, Mama Rosie stuck her head in the door, with Monty on her hip. "Lawd, look at the two of you. Anybody'd think y'all at a funeral 'stead of a wedding. Now, dry them tears, fix yo' makeup, and get ready to come down the aisle. It's time."
"Nothing like Mama to get us moving." Rosanna wiped her eyes.
Jimmy's daughters, Susanna and Savannah, preceded Jamaria down the aisle. His son, Jamie, escorted Jamaria, and stood beside his father as best man. When Rosanna entered with Papa Ben escorting her, there were few dry eyes in the church. Jimmy's brother performed the ceremony and said prayers for happiness of the couple.

Before the luncheon, Jimmy was speaking to Jamaria when they both overheard one of the guests, in a nearby Sunday school classroom.. "I don't know what he see in that big ol' clumsy thing, she ain't even pretty.
Jamaria started toward the room, but Jimmy touched her arm and whispered, "I got this."
He proceeded to the classroom. "Hello, ladies." He scrutinized them up and down. They both wore skirts so short and tight they left nothing to the imagination. "I overheard your remark and I'm sorry you felt the need to make such a remark at our wedding. But let me tell you what I find in Rosanna. She's a woman who is beautiful, both inside and out. A woman who would never make a remark such as you made. She's never make a derogatory remark about anyone. A woman who never feels the need to dress like a street hooker in the house of

God."

Jamaria, standing inside the door, heard the women gasp.

Jimmy continued, "I see a woman who never threw herself at a man, any man, because he's new in town, or single, or available, or might be willing to leave his wife. I fell in love with her for a lot of reasons, including those I mentioned. And I would never select either of you, or a lot of other women in your church for the same reasons. Let me finish with this: if you can't be happy for someone who is supposed to be your friend, you should leave right now. She doesn't need you here, and I don't want you here."

Jamaria, still standing inside the door, shocked by what Jimmy said, but happy.

He grinned at her as he came through the door. "Let's go find my bride. I've been away from her too long."

Two days after the wedding, Jamaria leafed through her mail, after putting the children to bed, when she found an envelope from the Social Security Administration. She had almost, but not quite, forgotten about them. In the back of her mind, she tried to convince herself she could be okay without the money. They could get by. She would still buy the children the clothes they needed, shoes, doctor's visits. How did other mothers do it; how would she be able stretch her paycheck any further?

The car always needed gas; Kacy needed things for school. She used cloth diapers for Monty, but he grew like a weed. Good thing she wore uniforms at work; thank God Mama Rosie didn't charge her for babysitting. How did other women manage?

Hesitating before opening the envelope: how disappointed will I be if the answer is no? She lay her head down across the envelope and said a silent prayer.
She grabbed the paring knife used to open envelopes and slit it. Taking the contents, she spread them out before her and began to read. Lots of information about Montre claiming Jamaria's unborn baby before his death. Information regarding his claim on Kacy with no evidence she had other parents, and his support of Kacy prior to his imprisonment. Jamaria was not eligible for benefits because she was not married to Montre, but the children were eligible.

"They said yes, they said yes," she shouted, jumped up, and danced across the kitchen. She grabbed a paper towel as tears dripped off her chin. "Wait," she said aloud to herself. "Let me read this again."

She ran her finger under the text as she reread the letter, grinning as she did. "I ain't never had this much money before. Money in the bank to take care of my babies. College, maybe." She said this aloud to herself again. She would have called Rosanna, but she and Jimmy were away on their honeymoon.

After her shower, Jamaria lay in bed, thinking about all the things she would do, now she had more money to help raise her children. But first a savings account, in case my children want to go to college. I don't want them having to work at a minimum wage job, like they mama.

She took the letter with her when she took Kacy to school the next day and showed it to Miss Mildred. "I jes wanted to show you what I got."

"What are you going to do with this money?"

"Well, I didn' sleep much las' night thinkin' 'bout this. I'm gon put most of it in my savin's, and I'm gonna start a savin's for my children. I hope someday they gon want to go to college. An' after all, this money for them."

"For their living expenses, too," Miss Mildred explained.

"I can jes 'bout make do on my money. I want to have somethin' for them when they grown, from they daddy. Won't be much to start, problly a hundred a month."

Mildred came from around the counter and hugged Jamaria. "You are the best person in the world a man could choose to leave Kacy with. He had to know when he left. No one is as unselfish as you are."

"No, Rosanna a better woman than I ever be. You should have heard Jimmy defending her at their wedding. I was 'bout to go and slap them two women, but he put them down with words that shamed them into leaving the church 'fore anybody even started eatin'." They laughed and Jamaria left, carrying Monty on her hip, headed to the bank.

ACKNOWLEDGEMENTS

There are multitudes who assisted with the preparation, ideas, inspiration, and encouragement in my writing this book of short stories. It would be impossible to mention all of them by name. But let me point out some of the most influential, not by name but by influence. It started many years ago and their names escape me. English teachers through the years indeed helped, although I don't always follow their teaching. Creative writing teachers also assisted.

Next, my family, my sons and their families, my grandchildren, my siblings--all of whom encouraged me beyond measure. Many very good friends whom I've known for more years than any of us want to remember, some I worked with and are also retired. We keep in touch!

I've made online friends through my critique group, Critique Circle, who 'tell it like it is' when doing critiques and taught me so much. They encouraged me more than I can say.

The local writers', Snake Nation Writers' Group, taught, and are still teaching me, so much more than I ever knew I didn't know! Sadly, we've lost members along the way, Jack, Vickie, and most recently, Morris, and we miss them. Their most helpful critiques are and will forever be missed. I thank all the members for their encouragement and willingness to continue even as I was ready to give it up--more than a few times.

AUTHOR BIOGRAPHY

B. R. Johnson was born in Brooks County, Georgia, as far south as you can go and still be in Georgia. She attended schools in the same county and graduated from college in the neighboring county, Valdosta State College. She likes to say she was on the 'finish by forty' plan. Three years later she received a Masters in Public Administration from Valdosta State University, the college having been upgraded since her graduation. She worked in a federal pilot pre-school program, before there were public kindergartens. When that program ended, she worked in the state welfare department, and after retirement, in a federal program at a local technical school with teenage girls and welfare recipients, for a total of over thirty years.

She has three sons, the last born when the first two were nineteen and seventeen. She currently lives alone, on the farm where she grew up, with a cat named Missy, next door to her sister and brother-in-law. She often sits with their dogs who bark at the cat even when they can't see her. The fourth boy in the dedication is a special nephew, Wayne, who grew up close to her oldest sons. "It was always like my sister and I had three sons each, rather than two and one at that time," she says.

There are many stories to choose from, but the stories in this book are completed fabricated.